# **FALL**

## THE KING BROTHERS SERIES

LOUISE ROSE

# CONTENTS

| | |
|---|---|
| Join my Newsletter! | vii |
| Prologue | 1 |
| Chapter 1 | 5 |
| Chapter 2 | 16 |
| Chapter 3 | 23 |
| Chapter 4 | 31 |
| Chapter 5 | 44 |
| Chapter 6 | 56 |
| Chapter 7 | 65 |
| Chapter 8 | 75 |
| Chapter 9 | 83 |
| Chapter 10 | 95 |
| Chapter 11 | 100 |
| Chapter 12 | 106 |
| Chapter 13 | 115 |
| Chapter 14 | 124 |
| Chapter 15 | 132 |
| Chapter 16 | 139 |
| Chapter 17 | 145 |
| Chapter 18 | 150 |
| Chapter 19 | 159 |
| Chapter 20 | 166 |
| Chapter 21 | 177 |
| Chapter 22 | 186 |
| Chapter 23 | 194 |
| Chapter 24 | 206 |
| Chapter 25 | 213 |
| Chapter 26 | 219 |
| Chapter 27 | 230 |

| Chapter 28 | 234 |
| Chapter 29 | 239 |
| Chapter 30 | 246 |
| Epilogue | 251 |
| Afterword | 255 |
| EXCLUSIVE EXTRA SCENE OF WHEN BLAKE PROPOSES TO IZZY… | 257 |
| 31. Bonus read of The Missing Wolf | 260 |
| 32. Bonus read of The Missing Wolf | 266 |
| 33. Bonus read of The Missing Wolf | 271 |
| 34. Bonus read of The Missing Wolf | 277 |

Fall © Copyright 2020 by Louise Rose

All rights reserved.

This is a work of fiction. Names, characters, places, brands, media, and incidents are either the product of the author's imagination or are used fictitiously.

The author acknowledges the trademark owners of various products, bands, and/or stores referenced in this work of fiction, which have been used without permission. The publication/use of these trademarks is not authorized, associated with, or sponsored by the trademark owners.

Photography by Sara Eirew

*Cover Design by Covers by Combs*

❦ Created with Vellum

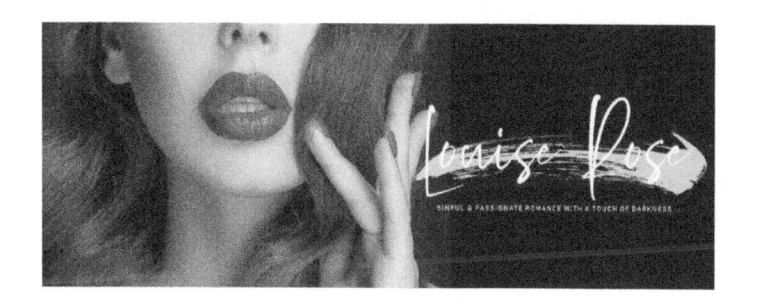

Click here to subscribe!

## DESCRIPTION

*When you run, how long does it take for your past to catch up with you?*

Harley King knows something is up when his sister's friend turns up unexpectedly and needs a place to stay.

When Harley lets Tilly live with him, he does not expect to fall for her smartass comments and her kind nature.

Tilly thought running from her past would keep her safe, but will Harley's past put her in danger?

Can the oldest King brother protect her when her secret comes out?

*Or will he walk away?*

**18+ due to violence, sexual scenes, and language.**
**With exclusive bonus scene.**

## **QUOTE**

*There are some people who could hear you speak a thousand words, and still not understand you. And there are others who will understand- without you even speaking a word.*
*-Yasmin Mogahed*

# PROLOGUE
TILLY

"Come on!" Emilia shouts at me, just as I spot Harley. Every part of me freezes when I see him; my mouth goes dry and fear fills me. He is in the cage, blood pouring down his face, two men are unconscious at his feet, and he is facing three other guys. Two of them are massive, and the other looks like he shouldn't be in the fight at all. There are hundreds of people around the cage, most shouting 'King,' but some are shouting other words I don't recognise. The noise is just that loud in here, but I can't move as I stare at Harley. I don't think I will ever forget seeing him this way, the way he looks so dangerous, but I know straight away that this is not who he is. Harley is the man who feeds my daughter when she wakes up at night, who brings me coffee in the morning. The man who cuts roses in his garden and puts them in my bedroom window. The man I find asleep in his study with a new book in his hands. That's my Harley, and this is the man he has been forced to be for too long."I see Sebastian at the bar," she shouts at me and tries to pull my arm, just as Harley rushes at two of the guys.

"Go, then," I say, unhooking my arm from hers and ignoring her when she tells me to come back.

I push through the people and duck under others who are jumping up and down. It doesn't take me long to get to the front of the crowd, with my body pushed against the cage wall.

Harley is struggling to fight the guys as two of the massive ones hold him down and the other hits his side. I feel sick as I see the almost defeated look he is wearing; this fight isn't fair. He can't die like this, not after everything this hell-hole has taken from him.

"HARLEY, FIGHT FOR ME!" I scream just as his bright-green eyes find mine.

## CHAPTER 1
TILLY

I can do this. I repeat to myself as the cab pulls up to the large, Victorian house I've seen in the photos my best friend sent me. The house is amazingly beautiful, with grey, stone walls and big, arched windows. It looks like something out of a damn fairy tale, not a house just outside a small, English village.

I forgot how cold England is compared to France, I think as I pull my coat closer around myself and wish the cab driver had put the heating on in the car.

"Here you go, love," the cab driver says as I snap out of my daze, and I hand him the money for the ride. The driver helps me get my one suitcase full of clothes out of the boot before driving off.

I hope Izzy is home. I think of my best friend who

lives here sometimes, when she isn't with her boyfriend, and I can't wait to see her. I remind myself it doesn't matter if she isn't in because undoubtedly one of her brothers can point me in her direction.

I straighten my back as I raise my hand to knock on the massive, wooden door, but it's suddenly pushed open by a handsome man. The man is wearing nearly all black-leather and has slightly long, messy black hair covering his stern looking face. He is struggling to hold two boxes under one arm, and my hand just misses his face as he dodges to the side, but, unfortunately, one of the boxes drop to the ground, with a sound like smashing glass.

"Shit," the man says in a deep voice.

"I'm so sorry," I mutter quickly, putting my hand down. Great first impression, almost hitting one of the King brothers in the face.

"Who are you?" the man asks bluntly, making me feel a little defensive. It's not like I meant to nearly hit him in the face and make him drop his box.

"I'm looking for Izzy," I say, matching his tone, and the man looks amused for a second. I'm confident he isn't going to tell me as he stares me down, holding onto his last box for dear life, when I hear Izzy shout behind him.

"Who's that?"

The man moves out of the way, and I see the welcome sight of Izzy running to me. She pushes the man out of the way, causing the last box to hit the floor with a bigger bang.

Izzy wraps herself around me in a big hug, which I return, barely holding in my tears at finally being able to see my best friend after so many years. Izzy is like the sister I never had, and damn, I've missed her.

"Tilly, what the hell are you doing here?" Izzy asks, pulling back to look at me. I look at her, too, noticing the changes. Not enough that I don't recognise her, but enough that I have to pause a second. Her hair is just as long and blond as before, but she has it up in a high ponytail with highlights running through it. The jumper and jeans she has on look made for her; she looks fantastic and happy. I know she is happy from her messages and phone calls, but seeing it is something else.

"Long story," I mutter, not wanting to ruin this moment by thinking about the reason I'm here unannounced and with only one bag. Even thinking of France leaves a sour taste in my mouth.

"I knew you would drop one," a deep, sexy-sounding voice says with a laugh as a man comes into the now- crammed hallway. Luckily, the house is big.

Damn, I can't take my eyes off this guy. He is tall, way over six feet, with long brown hair pulled together loosely at the back of his head. His startling green eyes, much like Izzy's, latch onto mine, and neither of us look away. He must be the oldest brother. Harley, if I remember right. I wish I had looked more at those photos Izzy sent me.

Harley looks a little confused as he asks, "Who is this?"

I don't say anything as I stare, and I swear I'm actually speechless as I check out his tight suit and the fantastic body filling it. Izzy clears her throat, making me look back at her after a long silence between us all. When I see her small smile, I grin because I'm so happy to see her again. Izzy pulls me into the hallway and out of the cold.

"I kind of need a place to stay. It's just for a few weeks until I find somewhere to rent. My family isn't moving here for two months, and it's a long story," I say to Izzy, who smiles as her green eyes widen. I'm happy she doesn't ask why, but I know she will the moment we are alone. As much as I trust her, I have no idea if I can even talk about everything yet. Even to Izzy.

"You can stay with me," she says, practically jumping up and down as she pulls me into a hug.

"Sorry, beauty, she can't. Allie's room is already

rented out, and I signed the contract. I forgot to tell you," a tall, blond man, who I recognise from Izzy's photos, says as he comes to stand next to Izzy while I look him up and down.

Damn, Izzy is a smart girl. He is hot with a muscular build and a small waist. He has this whole surfer look going on. Standing next to Izzy, they look like the perfect, California blond couple. Like they should be advertising surfboards or something.

"Good choice," I whisper to Izzy, making her laugh.

"She can stay here; Elliot's room is empty now, and we have others," Harley says, making everyone look toward him, including me. I don't think he ever stopped looking at me, and it's making me want to squirm under the pressure of his gaze. It's like he knows what I'm running from, and that scares me because no one can know. I ran from France, and from that man, so that people wouldn't know. I only need a place to stay for a little while until my family comes here, and I hope I'm strong enough to tell them. The thought of telling them anything is making me feel sick.

"I can stay in a hotel. I don't want to put anyone out," I say, knowing my tone sounds as nervous as I feel.

"I insist," Harley says, and I know he isn't asking now.

The man is powerful, and I'm smart enough to know I need to be somewhere safe for a little while just in case my past finds me. This could be a good place to hide, to make sure he doesn't find me. There's no doubt he will look into my old home and find out I was friends with Izzy. I'm just hoping none of Izzy's past can find her here.

"Well thanks, I'll pay rent, of course," I say, knowing that I have more than enough to pay for a little while. I am lucky my career is going well enough that I can dip into my savings, but I know long term, I'll need to plan things out.

"No, you won't. Izzy can sort out bed sheets for you," Harley says with one more look at me before walking away. I stand in shock for a second before realising I can't do that. I won't owe any man anything again.

"Hey! I will!" I shout at his back as he disappears out of the room, and I hear a chuckle from Harley in the kitchen, damn if his laugh isn't sexy, too.

"Well, it's nice to meet you, Tilly. Izzy has told me all about you since she came here," the man with the boxes says, holding out a hand for me to shake.

"You must be Elliot" I guess, remembering Izzy sending me photos of him next to a bike. I shake his hand with a friendly smile, which he returns, well almost.

"I'm Blake, but you've guessed that," Izzy's boyfriend says as I let go of Elliot's hand and look over at him.

"Yeah, from the fact that missy, over here, has sent me pictures of everyone. That was Harley, right?" I ask, gesturing to the kitchen area. I knew he was good-looking from the photos, but they didn't do him justice. He is hella hot in person, too.

"Yes, but tell me all about France and why you're here early." Izzy is practically bouncing up and down in excitement as she talks, making me laugh. I did miss her.

"Come on, then." I smile and mentally rerun my excuse for being here over and over in my head. It's not that I don't trust her, but I just can't tell her now. I hate lying, but I just can't tell her, or anyone. Not yet.

She takes my hand, leading me into a big living room area. It's fitted with three leather sofas and a big, old fireplace in the middle of the room. The room has light-brown walls, which match the dark wooden flooring throughout the house. There are two bookcases by the big window, filled with old-looking books, which I will have to have a look at, and the window shows off the impressive garden full of flowers.

Izzy pulls my arm, so I sit down next to her on one of the sofas, and she starts asking me questions, going a mile a minute. "So? Why did you come earlier? Why not wait? Are you okay? Why didn't you call me?"

"Beauty, maybe let her speak first," Blake interrupts with a smile at Izzy, who looks over at him as he sits on the sofa opposite us.

"Yes, sorry. I'm just so happy to see you. Video chats, phone calls, and emails aren't enough," Izzy says with a little blush, and I squeeze her hand.

"No, I get it, and it's just work. I have a new client, and it was easier to meet him here than fly back home," I lie, well slightly. I do have a new author who needs edits done and wants to meet, but I don't need to meet her to edit her book. I can always video call if needed.

"Right." Izzy raises an eyebrow at me, reminding me how she always knew when I was lying when we were younger. I know she is about to call me on it, but I shake my head softly and she squeezes my hand. I have no doubt she will demand to know everything later, but for now, she is letting it go.

"What do you do for work?" Blake asks into the silence of the room, changing the subject.

"I'm an editor. I work for myself, which is nice, and I've edited one book that's now an international bestseller," I say, smiling at the thought of how lucky I got with that author. It's been challenging to set up a client base, but I'm now fully booked for the next two months, and more and more orders are coming in. I also design book covers as an additional job, but it takes too much time when I would rather be editing.

"That's really impressive, Tilly," Blake smiles.

At that moment, a wave of sickness hits me hard, like it has been doing all damn week. I know I have to eat something or I will end up throwing up. I rip my bag open to find my ginger biscuits and pull out two. I glance up to see Izzy and Blake looking confused as I eat the second biscuit.

Damn, another lie; it's not like I can tell them the truth, so instead I say, "Sorry, I haven't eaten all day and, well, I get sick if I don't eat."

"Okay, no worries. How about I go and cook us some breakfast?" Blake asks, still looking a little worried as he and Izzy share a strange look.

"Thanks, I would like that," I answer, and he kisses Izzy on the head as he walks out.

"You going to tell me the truth now?" Izzy asks the moment the door shuts.

"No, and please just let me talk to you in my own time. I can't. I just can't," I say, breaking into a sob I can't control.

The last two weeks have been so hard to stay strong to get here. The last week has been a nightmare of finding my way here and making sure I couldn't be followed. My family must have been so worried when they saw the note I left them. I will call them soon, when I can tell them.

Izzy pulls me into her arms and says, "I don't care why you're here, but when you're ready, we will talk because I'm worried. I love you, Tilly, you're my sister, even if we're not related."

I nod, wiping my eyes as I pull away.

"I will, I promise." It's not like I can't tell her, as in a few months, she will guess. Izzy's phone rings, and she gets it out of her jean pocket.

"Luke, Tilly is here!" she says when she answers. "You remember Tilly? The girl I grew up with, the one who went to France?" She pauses to listen, then continues. "That's brilliant, and okay, tell him congrats. Yeah, that's great." There's another small pause before she responds again. "Okay, see you soon and I will, bye," she says, putting the phone down.

"Luke says hi." She beams at me. "Look, you met Elliot, right? Well, he just got news that he can open his new club this Saturday. Do you want to go? It will be great, and maybe you might meet someone," Izzy says with a wink.

But the thought of finding anyone at the moment only has the adverse effect of reminding me of my ex. "Sounds good," I say.

"Let's go and make sure Blake hasn't burnt the kitchen down." She laughs, holding a hand out for me.

## CHAPTER 2
TILLY

When we walk into the kitchen, I'm surprised by how modern it is with its light-wood cabinets and a massive, kitchen island with stools dotted around it. The appliances all look expensive, too, but my attention is drawn to Harley, who is sitting on one of the stools. I watch as he loosens his tie a little and shifts in his seat, almost like he knows I'm looking at him. He is concentrating on his paperwork so he doesn't notice us come in. I sit on a stool opposite him, and Izzy goes to help Blake cook.

Harley slowly looks up, and my attention fixates on his dazzling, green eyes. There isn't a touch of any other colour in them, just a pure-light green, and it's fascinating. I always thought Izzy's eyes were a pretty colour. Apparently, she got that from her father's side.

"I took your bag up to your room," he tells me after an awkward silence.

"Thanks. I'm still paying rent," I tell him firmly.

"No, you're not," he replies smoothly, almost like he expected me to say that as he puts his paperwork into his briefcase on the table.

"I am," I mutter louder, and he gives me an amused look. "You can try, and I will just send it back to you." He smirks, leaning back in his chair. Even when he's clearly challenging me, he is so damn attractive.

Someone clears their throat behind me, and I turn to see Blake handing me a plate. I accept it and see Izzy with a small smile on her face as she brings some sauces over to us.

"Why don't you offer her that part-time reception job? That way you both win," Blake offers as he walks to his own seat and holds a chair out for Izzy. That's sweet.

"Thanks, Blake, but I can still pay rent," I say, thinking about it. It's going to be bad enough being around Harley all the time, and I'm likely going to do something stupid like try to kiss him. Or even worse, blurt out how hot he is.

"That could work. I own a local gym and, two

days a week, I need a receptionist to help out. I would drive you there until you sort a car out," Harley says.

"All right. That could work around my other job," I say before thinking about it at all. It was like a natural reflex to say yes to him. I mentally sigh and take a bite of the scrambled eggs on toast. Damn, Blake can cook; lucky Izzy.

"What do you do?" Harley asks, standing up and putting his briefcase on one of the counters by the door.

I can't take my eyes off him, and I know I need to. Being attracted to my best friend's brother isn't a good idea at the moment. Plus, if my ex follows me here, I need to leave.

"I'm a book editor, it's a work at home job most of the time. I have a few clients I'm working with currently," I tell him as he gets a bottle of water from the fridge.

"Impressive, for someone your age," he comments, seeming more interested in looking at me now.

"It's impressive to own a successful business at your age," I compliment him back, because it is. He can't be much older than I am, and he owns his own business as well as looking after his brothers and sister, from what Izzy has told me.

"I have to get to the office. I hope you settle in well," he says before walking past me. I swear I feel his fingers lightly touching my back as he passes me, but I could be imagining things. Or hoping.

"I'll be back tonight, Iz. Are you staying over?" Harley asks from the doorway.

"No, I can't because I have class in the morning and I can't miss it. I'll be back tomorrow after class for a few days," she says, turning slightly to wink at me.

"All right, Luke and I can keep your guest busy tonight." Harley sighs, sounding like he would rather be doing anything else.

"Forget it, I'm tired. I'll just go to bed early," I say a little too harshly, and I know it's not really much to do with him but more of my hate for being in this situation. Harley picks up on my tone straight away and smiles.

"See you tonight, Tilly." With that, he walks out of the room and we hear the front door shut not long after. Did he not just listen to me?

"You'll like Luke, he has a thing for tattoos, like you," Izzy says around eating her eggs. I remember Izzy telling me Luke is her younger brother and that the twins, Elliot and Sebastian, are only a little older than her.

"I don't have a massive thing for tattoos," I protest.

"You have four, and one is all the way from the top of your back to your bum," she points out, and she is right. That's my biggest tattoo, and it's a mixture of small vines and flowers of different colours. It took over a month for them to do, as it's so detailed. My other tattoos are much smaller, like the one in the middle of my wrist, which is a fox, like my last name, Fox. All my siblings have one in the same place, and it only fills me with regret that I couldn't speak to them before I left. That I couldn't explain why I need to hide from my ex, their best friend.

"Well, you have one, too," I whisper, knowing some of her brothers don't know Luke tattooed her thigh a while ago.

"What's your real name? As I'm guessing Tilly is a nickname?" Blake asks as we all finish eating.

"I don't tell people my name, it's horrible, so it's Tilly," I tell him.

"What happens when you get married? Everyone will hear it then," he replies, picking up the empty plates and taking them over to the side.

"It's not that bad anyway," Izzy says, laughing when I glare at her.

"It's horrible, and I'm not getting married

anytime soon ... so no one will know," I say, making them both laugh.

"Anyway, let me show you to your room," she says.

I stand up and take my empty plate to Blake as he turns the water on.

"Okay," I reply as I smile at my oldest friend. I didn't realise how much I missed her because she has always been more like a sister to me than a friend. I love my brothers, all three of them, and I've felt the same kind of love for Izzy.

Izzy leads me up the giant, wooden stairs and to a long corridor. There are quite a few doors and a little personality, as it's all filled with paintings of flowers and beaches by the looks of it. I can see another staircase at the end of the corridor, and I wonder what's on the next floor. Izzy leads me straight to the right and opens a door. The bed is the first thing I see as it's huge and takes up most of the room with its big, wooden frame, and there is a large wardrobe in the one corner as well. There's a matching wooden box at the end of the bed and a chest of drawers under the window.

"This one has its own bathroom, so that's why he gave it to you rather than a spare room." Izzy opens the door to show me a small en-suite shower room with a toilet.

"I have to pay rent now, this room is incredible," I say, looking around and seeing the cardboard boxes in the corner with a bed store's company name on them. The bed must be pretty new.

"Harley is the most stubborn man I've ever met, but what did you think of him?" Izzy asks me, a slightly calculating look running over her face.

"Handsome, smart, and, well, kind to invite me here, but he clearly isn't aware of how stubborn I can be," I say as I cross my arms, and Izzy chuckles.

"I guess not." Izzy laughs, coming over and turning serious for a second. "You sure you're okay?" she asks as she pulls me into a tight hug.

"I am now, that's all that matters," I whisper, and I feel her tense, pulling back to look at me.

"Right. Well, I have to get back to my apartment to study, so I'll see you tomorrow?" she asks.

"Tomorrow." I nod.

With another hug, she lets me go and shuts the door behind her. Finally, I let the tears fall; not because I'm upset, but because I know I'm safe, for now.

## CHAPTER 3

HARLEY

"Elliot, leave," I say as I hold the door to the basement open, and my dad looks over at me while my loud voice echoes around the room.

Elliot is twelve, fucking, years old, and Dad is beating the shit out of him. Elliot raises his head off the mat as Dad's fist stops mid-air at my comment, and I know I'm about to get fucking hell for stopping this.

They pull apart as Dad stands up, as does Elliot, but far more scarily. His dark hair is matted to his head with sweat, and blood is pouring out of his nose onto the blue mat on the floor. Elliot's arms hold his chest, and I know I will have to make sure nothing is broken later. I'm sure Dad's 'training' could have been worse if I hadn't come back sooner. I only went out on a bloody date for one night. I should have known Dad would take the chance to teach them without me here to stop him. He always *does this because he knows I will stop him, and then he will have to punish me instead, which I think he is getting bored of doing since I've gotten older. And stronger.*

*"Go on, little boy," Dad taunts, walking away as Elliot rushes past me out the door, not making any eye contact.*

*I will have to call the school tomorrow and tell them he isn't coming in for a few days until his ribs, or whatever the fuck else Dad has done, have healed. The fact he moved so quickly out of the room gives me hope that nothing is too wrong.*

*"You never learn, Harley. Always protecting them like the little shit you are," Dad says, walking over to me as I shut the door behind me. The last thing I need is for the kids to hear any of this.*

*Dad grabs his bottle of whatever and drinks a load while he watches me, clearly calculating something.*

*"Tomorrow, you're fighting for me. You won't lose," he tells me before pouring himself another drink.*

*"What?" I ask in horror as I hope he isn't thinking what I'm thinking.*

*"Don't act fucking dumb, Harley. You're the best I've seen when you fight those boys I find for you. Your brothers can't last two seconds," he spits out.*

*"That's because they are against adult men who fight for a living. They are kids, Dad. Don't you give a shit about us?" I shout.*

*"You will do it, and they will learn."* Dad shrugs, drinking more.

*"Are you not even going to answer my question? Are we just here to win fights for you in The Cage? Is that the only reason you kept us around after Mum left?"*

*"Don't talk about that bitch,"* he says, throwing his glass into the wall. I don't even flinch as it smashes.

*"Tomorrow,"* he says, walking past me, and the reek of alcohol nearly makes me choke as he walks past. He stops as he opens the door and looks back at me.

*"After all, it's your birthday, Son. Don't say I don't care. I remembered."* He chuckles to himself as I hear the door slam behind me, and I pray I make it out alive for no other reason than my brothers need me.

"Man, just go and knock on her door." Luke bumps my shoulder as he carries two pizza boxes into the lounge, and I snap out of the memory.

I have no idea why I'm thinking about it now. Isn't it bad enough my memories haunt me when I sleep? I continue to pace, getting more pissed that Tilly hasn't come downstairs since Izzy left earlier today. She must be hungry, and I'm ignoring the part of me that is begging for a chance to stare at her more. The red-haired siren is going to be the death of me, I think as I walk out of the lounge and head upstairs.

I stop when I'm standing outside her bedroom,

which is opposite mine. I groan internally, considering how it's a bad idea to have her so close. I could have given her the guest room next to Izzy, but I'm a selfish bastard who wants to see her first in the morning, even if I can't be the one she wakes up next to. I would be no good for a girl like her. I'm too messed up to offer her anything.

I knock a few times before the door is opened by a freshly showered Tilly. Her red hair is down, and she is wearing a silky green pyjama shirt and trousers. The colour complements her pale skin and her hair, making her more bloody beautiful. I swear this siren was sent here to tease me.

"Do you need something?" she asks me, raising one perfect eyebrow in suspicion as her eyes drop to my body before meeting my eyes again. She, apparently, caught me checking her out. Not that I care if she realises.

"Dinner is here, come downstairs," I reply.

"No." She goes to shut the door, and I stop it with my foot before pushing it open a little more so I can see her face in the dark room.

"That's rude," I comment, almost amused by her need to get away from me so quickly.

"Me? You didn't say please, so you're clearly the rude one here," she says, hiding a small smile.

"You must be hungry." I shrug off her comment, not wanting to admit she might be right.

"Nope, I wouldn't want to bother you." She crosses her arms, making her large chest bounce up. It takes me way too long to pull my gaze up to her eyes, and she glares at me.

"Please come and eat with us. If you don't, I swear I'll put you over my shoulder and carry you downstairs," I tell her, meaning every word. I don't like the idea of her sitting up here hungry and alone.

"You only had to say please," she huffs, slipping past me and walking toward the stairs as I stare at her fantastic ass.

"I don't say please often, siren, you might as well just do as I ask," I say, and she looks over her shoulder at me before she laughs. I really won't ask her nicely again. Clearly, the little siren isn't going to listen to me.

I run my hands over my face, looking away from Tilly's ass as I try to calm the fucking hard-on I have down. I fucking love it when women don't act like cowards, but I can't have this one. Man, she must be four years younger than me, and my sister's best friend to boot.

"Well, hello there," Luke says to Tilly as she walks into the lounge. I walk in as he openly checks her out before looking at my face and smartly looking sheepish. I try not to glare at him, but it doesn't work. I already want to get him to leave somehow. What the hell is wrong with me?

"You must be Luke," she says before sitting on the opposite sofa to Luke. I don't even want to admit how relieved I am that she chose not to sit by him. I take the seat next to her, despite her glare in my direction.

"You must be Tilly, is that short for anything?" Luke asks, flipping the channel to music he likes.

"Maybe, but that's like asking a woman's age; I won't tell you," she jokes, eyeing the pizza.

"Help yourself, there's a four-cheese pizza and a pepperoni one." I wave a hand.

Luke thinks about what she says before saying, "It can't be that bad of a name."

"It is." She laughs, taking three pieces of the four-cheese one, and I help myself to a mixture of both.

We eat in a comfortable silence before Luke starts asking more questions.

"So why isn't your family here?"

"It's complicated. We are all moving here in three months anyway. I just needed to leave a little early," she says, shifting slightly in her seat and keeping her face blank. Most people wouldn't think she was lying. That's one thing I've always been good at, spotting when people lie, and I know the siren is lying right now.

"Why?" Luke asks, not caring how Tilly tenses and looks away.

"She doesn't have to answer that," I point out.

"So I've eaten, and, now, I'm going to bed." Tilly stands, moving surprisingly quick out of the room. I have to jog to catch her at the bottom of the stairs.

"Wait," I say, and she halts on the stairs, turning to face me.

"We are going to watch a movie if you want to stay. I promise to stop Luke from being a nosy fucker." I grin.

I step a little closer to the stairs, and she watches me as I gently push a stray curl behind her ear, pulling my hand back as I realise what I just did. Fuck, I shouldn't have done that. Her impossibly blue eyes widen, and her cheeks flush red.

"I'm tired, so thanks but goodnight," she stutters some of her words and quickly runs away from me up the stairs.

What the fuck was I thinking, standing so close to her or touching her soft, fucking, hair? I don't do relationships. I walk into the lounge and sit down.

"Bro, she is hot," Luke says, leaning back on the sofa and watching me for some kind of reaction.

I look over at him, noticing how he has grown up recently, looking older than I've ever seen him.

"Watch it," I say, opening a beer that Luke has placed on the table.

"You like her," he says, looking a little shocked.

"No, I don't." I end the conversation because, honestly, I need to get her out of my head. She reminds me of things I can't have because of my past, like a happy, normal future.

# CHAPTER 4
## TILLY

"I forgot how frigging awesome you always look," I compliment my best friend as she pulls down her tight, black, sparkling dress, which shows off all her curves. Her blond hair is curled down her back like mine, and we are both wearing a little makeup as I don't like it, and she doesn't need it.

"Coming from the red-headed bombshell." She shakes her head at me with a grin.

I walk over and stand next to the mirror with her. I'll admit, I do look good today. I'm wearing a tight-feeling, green dress that dips to show off my breasts. The dip stops just before my belly button, and you can see the curves of my breasts, which I'm sure have gotten bigger during the last two weeks. I know I won't be able to wear a dress like this for much longer, but my stomach looks as flat as usual now.

"Come on, picture time," Izzy says, pulling me to her and taking several photos of us on both our phones. My phone rings in the middle of a picture, and I'm quick to ignore it, but I know Izzy saw my mum's name.

"Why are you ignoring your mum? And deleting your Facebook and Twitter?" she asks, placing her hands on her hips. Izzy loves my mum, like most people, including me, do, and she must think I'm awful to ignore her calls. If I tell my mum where I am, she will come here and he will follow.

"Not tonight, no questions please," I whisper, guilt, and a slight bit of fear, stuck in my throat. It's not that my family has done anything wrong, but I have more than them and myself to think of now. Everything has changed, and the one person I wish was here, is my mum.

"Tomorrow, I want answers, Tilly. I'm worried about you," she tells me firmly, placing her hand on my arm.

I cover her hand with mine, looking at our painted nails, which match. I remember when we both tried to paint our nails like our mums when we were seven. Let's just say that more nail polish got on our fingers than our nails.

"No promises . . . but I will try to tell you some stuff. There's a lot to tell," I say, knowing I didn't tell her anything that happened in France this past year. I should have, but I was stupid enough not to because Izzy had been so busy and stressed with all the changes in her life. And then, there was the car accident.

"Tomorrow," Izzy says with a stern look, making me smile. It doesn't suit her, acting all serious, and she ends up laughing at me.

We finish getting ready before going down to the kitchen. I slip on my silver heels, giving me a little height boost, but I don't need it. Izzy's black heels are far higher than mine because she is so much shorter than I am. I kind of wish I was her height sometimes, it's difficult to find a man as tall as me, or taller. And I like taller men, like Harley.

*Nope, stop that thought.*

We walk down the stairs, with Izzy grinning at me the whole time. She looks so happy to have me here, but then, I never expected less from Izzy. You know, sometimes in life, you have that bond with someone who isn't blood? Well, that is my bond with Izzy, a sisterly bond.

"I'm a lucky man." Izzy stops by the door to the kitchen as Blake walks out, his words slow and seductive. He walks straight to her and slides an arm around her waist, pulling her to his chest. The look he is giving her should be illegal, and Izzy is a very lucky woman.

"I'll meet you in there," Izzy says as she giggles at something Blake whispers to her, and I look away as they kiss.

I walk around them toward the kitchen, wishing, in a way, I had met as good guy as Blake seems to be. My ex is anything but good, and I thought I was crazy in love with him. *Look where that got me*, I think.

My gaze finds Harley's first, like he is the only person in the room, and I struggle to pull my gaze away. I check out his tight, black shirt and black jeans, which make him look bloody amazing. His dark-brown hair is tied back, like usual, showing off his bright-green eyes, which seem brighter as he takes me in from head to toe. I do eventually look away, the pressure of his gaze making me nervous, and see Luke leaning against the sink, smirking at me and then looking at Harley.

"What do you think?" I twirl a little for everyone who's staring at me. Well, just for Harley. In fact, I don't even know why I'm asking if he likes what I'm wearing. I guess some part of me just wants to hear his answer.

"I love the dress." Luke playfully winks at me, but Harley never answers.

I try not to let it annoy me, but it does a little. As handsome as Luke is with his tattooed arms, well-trimmed beard, and tight clothes, which show off his massive build, he isn't Harley. There's just something about Harley that makes me unable to stop thinking about him.

Izzy and Blake come into the room looking rosy-cheeked, and Izzy's lipstick is a little askew, but it doesn't matter as she seems so happy. It's hard to actually look away from them both, with how comfortable they look with each other. I have to admit to myself that I'm a little jealous because I wish I had met a good guy like Blake instead of where my life ended up taking me.

Izzy lets go of Blake's arm and walks over to stand next to me.

"Let's go," Izzy says, hooking her arm with mine as she leads me out of the kitchen, and I feel Harley's eyes on my back. I can't explain how I know he is looking at me, but I can.

"Come on, man, we're leaving," I hear Luke say, and I turn to see him pat Harley's back as he is still watching me silently, like I knew he was.

The taxi bus is already outside when we leave the house, and the taxi driver is holding the door open as he speaks on his phone. The middle-aged man nods at us, his eyes spending way too long watching Izzy and me.

"Eyes up here, mate, if you know what's good for you," Blake warns him as I get into the taxi with Izzy.

The driver says something I can't hear, but the tone is easy to understand, he sounds scared, and I don't blame him one bit. The King brothers and Blake look a scary lot altogether.

After everyone is in, I sit in the taxi bus quietly as I watch the town. It's a quiet village with beautiful, grey stone houses built around a large river. We pass the massive, grey stone bridge I saw on the way in. It is arched and looks very old. I gaze behind me, and my eyes lock with Harley, who is staring at me.

I can't pull my eyes away until we stop outside a building in the middle of the town. I can't see much other than the name outlined in lights and the front door. There is also a massive queue in front of the club, and they aren't letting many people in so it must be busy. I can't say I've been to many clubs because we lived in a small town in France, and I would have to travel to the central city to go out. By the time I turned eighteen, I was too busy with setting up my business with my brother and editing books for low rates to build a client base.

And then I met him, and there was no way he would let me go out to clubs like this. He never let me go out at all, not unless he was at my side and watched my every move. I'm going on twenty . . . yet as I look at the club, I've never felt older or more lost.

The sound of Luke sliding the door of the taxi bus open snaps me from my thoughts.

We all get out, and I follow Luke up to the club and to the bouncer. The bouncer grins at Luke when he sees him, and they do a manly hug and handshake–clearly, they know each other–before he lets us in. The club is boiling hot, and the loud music fills my ears straight away when we walk in.

*Thank god for my small dress.*

I find myself staring around at all the shiny surfaces and the bottles lining the wall behind the bar. It's a very well decorated club, and it's clear someone has spent a lot of money on it. It's not trashy at all. There is a shining dance floor, with stools around it and people sitting on them, talking as they drink cocktails. There's also a glass balcony overlooking everything. While I'm staring around the room, I see Harley walking toward the bar, and several girls turn their heads to watch him. I can't blame them, the man is hotter than any guy I've seen in a long time. There's something about him that makes you not want to look away, and, in my case, makes me want to be near him. He looks back, like he can feel me watching, and I pull my gaze away.

"I can't believe we never went clubbing, you remember when we were fifteen and it's all we wanted to do? We used to beg Grayson to take us, but he wouldn't," Izzy says with a laugh, referring to my oldest brother.

"I remember him walking out of the room and telling us to leave him alone, he was a moody asshole back then."

Izzy laughs and links her arm in mine as we follow Luke upstairs to the balcony. The moment the balcony doors shut, the light music from up here can be heard, and it's clear the room is soundproof. Elliot is at the bar with some men in suits. He waves at us as we come in.

I sit on one of the leather couches facing the dance floor with the others. Izzy and Blake sit together on one, and Luke sits next to me. I don't know how long I sit, quietly watching the people dance, losing themselves to the music and wondering if that's what I need, to lose myself to music and just forget everything for one night. To just lose myself and my past.

A waitress dressed all in black, with ample cleavage hanging out of her tight top, comes over, eying up both Luke and Blake, but Blake doesn't seem to notice her as he talks to Izzy. That's a sign of a good man right there.

"Can I get you all anything?" she asks with her

eyes eating up Luke, and he leans back on the sofa, his arms wide.

"Shots all around, tequila and a beer for me, gorgeous," Luke says, making her giggle. She might as well lie naked on the table for him at this rate.

"What do you want?" Luke asks, and Izzy replies before I can say anything.

"Tilly is a classic Vodka and Coke girl." Which would usually be true, but not tonight.

"I'll have a vodka and Coke," I say to the waitress, and she takes down all our orders before leaving to make them.

I quickly get up to follow her, but Izzy asks before I can walk away, "Where are you going?"

"Oh, I don't want ice so I'm just going to check she doesn't put any in," I say, making up another lie and wanting to kick myself for it.

She is going to hate me when I can finally tell her, and I feel like the lies I've told since I've come here are just adding up. I never used to lie, and now look at me, I even lie to myself every morning by saying it's going to be okay when that can't be true.

"Right," Izzy says, with a look that makes me wonder what she is thinking and hoping she can't see straight through me like she always used to be able to.

"Be right back," I say before walking over to the bar. I call the girl over, who smiles at me.

"Did you want something else? Elliot said all of your drinks are on the house," she says, looking behind me to my table. At Luke, I'm guessing.

"No, I just remembered I have to drive somewhere tomorrow so no vodka in the coke," I tell her, and she gets out her notepad, writing it down.

"Okay, sugar cups." She winks at me as I flush red. My hand travels to my stomach without thought, and I look back at the table to see Izzy staring at me. I try to avoid her gaze as I walk back to the table, noticing Elliot has joined us.

"Hey, Elliot, right? Nice to see you again, and I promise not break any of your stuff this time," I say.

Elliot nods at me with a slight laugh.

"It's cool, I didn't need the stuff in those boxes," he says, but I'm sure he is just saying that to make me feel better.

"Where's Harley?" Elliot asks Luke, who shrugs as he replies.

"Downstairs at the bar, he is in a weird-ass mood this week."

"Is Allie going to be here soon?" Izzy asks Elliot, whose hard face softens under her name. I know Allie and Elliot are dating, and they are madly in love. Izzy told me they went through a lot and that

Elliot is a different man since he has been with Allie. Apparently, they are perfect for each other.

"Yeah, soon. I'm going to get her. I just needed to chat with some staff."

"Go on, then, I want to see my bestie." She grins. I heard so much about this Allie from Izzy that I'm looking forward to meeting her.

"All right, you're such a demanding pain in the ass." Elliot chuckles before leaving. It's not long before the drinks arrive, and I quickly take my Coke off the tray for the waitress.

"So . . . shots to finally meeting the famous Tilly. Seriously, Izzy has told us everything about you but don't worry, most of it is good." Luke hands me a shot and winks.

*Shit, how am I going to get out of this?*

"To Tilly," he says, pouring his shot back while I pretend to drink mine and then I stand, pouring it into my coke before anyone sees.

"Thanks for this." I lift the empty shot and put it on the table before walking over to the window overlooking the dance floor.

I pretend to watch the people dancing on the floor for a while, but my thoughts are swimming with worries about my future and what I'm going to do now. This wasn't how I planned my life. This wasn't what I planned at all, but what can I do? I can't get out of this one no matter how much I may want to.

I look over to see Harley at the bar, just as he downs another drink. I don't know why I'm pretending a guy like him would look twice at me. The moment he knows, he is going to walk away. I wouldn't even want to put the responsibility of me on his shoulders, he is clearly a good guy.

"I'm going to dance," I say suddenly, deciding I just need to relax and stop staring at a man I can't have.

"Me, too," Izzy says, standing up.

Izzy and Blake follow me out from the balcony and down the stairs to the lower floor. I filter through the barely-dressed bodies of people before closing my eyes and letting the music relax me. It's a fast song I don't recognise, but it's easy to move to.

I don't know how long I'm dancing with my eyes closed when I feel large, warm hands grabbing my hips and pulling me back to an impossibly-hard chest. I stiffen in reaction as fear claws up my throat.

*It can't be Daniel.*

"Only me, siren. I wanted a dance," Harley's deep, throaty voice whispers next to my ear, and my body instantly relaxes into his arms.

I open my eyes to see Izzy dancing near me with Blake, but, thankfully, he is distracting her. I turn to face him slowly, and he keeps his hands on my sides the whole time, as if he doesn't want to let me go far; I know I feel the same.

I know I will regret this in the morning. I will regret letting any man get close to me again. But Harley King isn't just any man. I start swaying my hips and I wind my arms around his neck as my body takes control, the beat of the music is slow, and he knows how to move to it. We are pressed so tightly together that I can smell his incredible scent even with the scent of beer on his breath.

His body is hard but soft as we melt together. I forget who, and where, we are as I gaze up into his eyes and lean on my tiptoes, pressing a kiss to his shocked lips. I pull away so I can lean up to his body to whisper into his ear.

"Thanks for a memory I won't forget. I needed to escape for a while."

I pull away from his warm body as I quickly move off the dance floor. Finding my way outside, I hail a taxi waiting outside the club. I send a text to Izzy, telling her I've gone home as I don't feel well.

Only when I'm on my way back to the house do I relax, remembering how perfect Harley tasted and how, at least, I have one good memory from the last few months to remember. Even if it can never happen again.

## CHAPTER 5
### HARLEY

"How did you do that?" my girlfriend Hazel asks as I pull on my shirt while she watches.

I turn to look at her as I pull my jeans up. Hazel is pretty in that classic, brown-haired, blue-eyed, girl-next-door kind of way. We've been dating for a year now, and it still shocks me that I've kept my home life a secret from her. I only lie to her because I care for her. Or that's what I keep telling myself. The truth is, she is my first girlfriend and I'm in love with her. I love how simple she is, how she only wants me and nothing else. It's easy being with her.

"Just that boxing class I told you about," I say, wanting to flinch at the lie that comes out smoothly from my mouth.

Hazel smiles, wrapping the bedsheet around her as she walks over to me. Hell, I'm a sixteen-year-old lad *and I can't keep my eyes off her even after I've just had her.*

*"Why don't I stay at yours tonight?" She pouts, and I sigh. I don't like letting her down, I never have, but this is just how it is now.*

*"Not tonight. I've got to go," I say, walking closer to her and kissing her forehead as she sighs.*

*"Why won't you let me stay at yours? It's always rushed with you, and then you leave," she asks me.*

*"We could book a hotel and stay overnight together." I avoid her question.*

*"Harley," she grumbles.*

*"I have to go," I say, not looking at her again as I leave her house and head to my car. I drive back to my home in a few minutes, and I know the boys are hiding in their rooms as Dad's car is here.*

*When I walk in, I hear the music blasting downstairs in the basement, and I try to make it to the stairs without them hearing me. I don't want to deal with this shit tonight. Just one night off would be fucking great. I know Seb is out with Luke tonight, but I couldn't find Elliot to tell him I was going out.*

*"Come on, boy, your Dad has been waiting," Arthur, my dad's best friend and business partner, says, coming out of the kitchen with some girl about my age wrapped around him.*

*Arthur has a cruel expression, which matches his*

*personality, and he's wearing an expensive-looking suit. His brown hair is cut short, and his blue eyes watch me like I'm about to run. I bet he would love it if I did, but he knows I won't. I won't leave my brothers with my asshole of a father.*

*"Okay," I grind out, letting go of my tight grip on the bannister and following Arthur down the stairs to the basement.*

*I'm a little taken aback to see three women, naked and dancing on the bar as music blasts through the room. I catch Elliot's guilty face as he sits by our dad in the middle of the room on one of the sofas. There's a woman sitting on Elliot's lap, kissing his neck, and I swallow the urge to vomit at the knowledge Elliot doesn't have much choice right now. You know what . . . fuck it, it's worth a beating to stop this from happening. He is too young for this, and it's not like I can call the police or social services to help. The local police live in The Cage, and the last social worker who came here suddenly became very rich and disappeared.*

*"Elliot, get the fuck upstairs," I say, glaring at my father as Elliot slides the woman off his lap, jumping up and rushing out.*

*Elliot gets it worse than Sebastian, and I have no idea why. It's bad enough Elliot is the image of our father, the two look so alike.*

*"Harley, no need to ruin all the fun," he says, and the*

*few guys in the room laugh at my father's poor joke. No part of this is fun, it's just messed up.*

*Arthur smirks at me as he sits at the bar, watching, and I pull my gaze away from him back to my father.*

*"Come, sit," he commands, nodding his head to the empty seat next to him.*

*I tighten my fists and sit next to him on the sofa like he asks because I know he will just get Elliot back if I don't. My father is dressed in a shirt that's open, showing off how much of a big guy he is. Luckily for me, I follow our father in that trait. I'm nearly as big as he is with all the training. The fights are few and far between and much more for my father's sick pleasure than the money I earn.*

*The minute I sit down, the slut who was flung over Elliot sits on my lap with her wandering hands. The smell of stale cigarettes and cheap perfume fills my nose, making me want to be sick. When I look up, seeing her dazed eyes and the injection marks scattered all down her arms, I feel sicker.*

*"Tell me, how is that pretty girlfriend of yours?" Arthur asks with a smirk as his hand travels up the short skirt of the woman he is with. She has similar marks on her arms, and I'm betting my father is the one who gives her all the drugs she wants.*

*"Fine." I grit my teeth, hating that he even knows what she looks like.*

*"Pamela, baby, take my boy and teach him how to look*

*after that sweet girlfriend of his," Dad says, stroking the arm of Pamela, who is on my lap. Sickness fills me when I process his words.*

*"No."*

*I push away from the sofa to stand up, making Pamela jump off my lap, and my father stands too. There's a strange silence in the room, just the music playing, but no one says a word. I know better than to show him up like this, but I don't want to fuck whoever he wants anymore. I can't do that and keep dating Hazel. It's not fair to her. He comes close to my face as he grins in a cocky way.*

*"You'll fuck her, or I'll get your brothers to," he says, knowing I will protect them no matter what.*

*"When you're done, I have someone for you to fight. I don't want him walking after, so be ready." He squeezes my shoulder with a warning in his eyes, and I know he will beat the shit out of me if I say no.*

*I look over to the stupid woman who must be ten years older than me. I don't want to do this. I don't want to cheat on Hazel. I don't have any choice. But there is one choice I do have, and that's breaking up with Hazel tomorrow and then never having a relationship again.*

*I don't deserve that kind of happiness, and my brothers need me.*

I wake up in a hot sweat as the memories of that fucking night wash over me, making me feel sick. *What the fuck is causing me to remember this shit?* It takes me a few times of rubbing my face to remind myself I'm in a better place. That I'm not a kid anymore, but the resolve of staying away from women and anything serious has never left me. I avoid girls my own age in case I fall for them, in case I like them too much. Older women are just easier, and usually mean I can walk away in the morning. No matter how shit that makes me. I do tell them it's never more than one night and, usually, they want the same thing.

I roll out of bed and head to the shower, turning it to a hot temperature to wash away the thoughts of anything I remember. I dress in a suit and try to think of today, and then realise I'm taking Tilly to my work today.

*Why the fuck am I nervous?*

I haven't been able to get that kiss out of my head since Saturday, but all day Sunday, I couldn't get her alone to talk to because Izzy was there.

I brush my long hair back into a knot at the back of my head, and I finish straightening my tie. I have two Skype meetings today and three other meetings about new classes joining the gym. It's going to be a long-ass day.

I look at myself in the mirror, noticing all the changes since I was seventeen years old. These days, I don't look like my twenty-four-year-old age, I look in my thirties. That's why I have no fucking clue why someone as hot as Tilly would kiss me when she should be with someone her own age. Fuck, I know four years isn't a big age difference but, to me, it feels like it.

I come out of my room at the same time Tilly does. I flash her a smile as I check out her outfit. Fuck me, she looks like a sexy librarian. She is wearing tight, little black slacks and a fitted, white shirt. Hell, she even has these black glasses on. Shit, all I'm going to be thinking about today is fucking her over my desk with just those glasses on. Maybe she could keep the heels on, too.

"Morning, I like the glasses," I say in a deeper voice than usual as my palms start itching for me to touch her.

"Morning to you, too. Thanks, I only wear them when I work." She blushes, tucking a stray piece of hair behind her ear as the rest is up in a tight bun.

I step a little closer, just so I can smell her sweet, fruity smell, and whisper, "You should always wear them, they make you more spectacular than usual."

"Oh," she whispers back, as we stare at each other.

The door down the hall bangs open as Luke comes out of his room, and I step back.

"Good morning," he shouts, way too cheerful for first thing in the morning.

"We're leaving in an hour," I say to Tilly, but I leave before I do something stupid, like press her against the wall and kiss her. I have to adjust myself in this tight suit, and Luke notices with a laugh before he walks down the stairs. I'm lucky he doesn't say anything.

I hear Tilly following us, but I force myself not to look back. I need to get as far away from her as possible. I head straight to the espresso machine and turn it on, sliding a cup underneath it.

"Do you want one?" I ask Tilly as she hovers in the doorway.

"Nope. I can buy my own food later," she says as she nervously looks around.

"You can eat with us, the cleaners are paid to do a weekly shop and we never eat it all," I tell her.

"Are you sure?" she asks, and I nod.

"So, coffee?" I ask again.

"No, I'll just have some juice and toast. I don't like coffee," she says.

"Who doesn't like coffee?" I chuckle, making her smile.

"Seriously, I couldn't live without the stuff," Luke says, taking the cup from the espresso machine as I glare at him. "Dude, I'm in a rush today." He shrugs and starts drinking. I hope the coffee burns his mouth, the fucker.

"Help yourself, Tilly." I wave my hand at the kitchen.

"Sorry, guys, I have to go. I've overslept and have an early class," Luke says, grabbing an apple and downing his coffee.

"Bye," I say as I get a bottle of juice from the fridge and hand it to Tilly while she puts her toast in the toaster.

I eat a few grapes and an apple as she eats her toast in silence. An awkward kind of silence, which I don't like. After I make myself a new coffee, I know I need to say something. I don't want it to be like this between us.

"So . . . today I'll show you how to work everything. Basically, I just need you to answer the phones and answer any questions people may have," I explain. My other secretary does all the paperwork, so I don't need her to fill in there.

"All right, I can do that," she replies.

"I have a few meetings today, so I can't be interrupted unless it's important," I tell her, and she nods.

"So family only?" she asks as she eats her toast. I want to offer her butter, but she doesn't seem to care.

"Yeah, Sebastian, my brother who you haven't met, is my business partner and he will be there today," I say, drinking more of my coffee.

"Izzy told me about him. Elliot's twin, right?"

"Yes." I nod.

"Is he the married one?" she asks as she finishes her food.

"Yeah, Maisy is his wife, and Jake is their son. They have another one on the way who I can't wait to meet," I respond.

"How far along is she?" she asks, looking at me now as that seems to catch her attention for some reason.

"About four months, I believe," I answer and then drink the rest of my coffee, looking back at Tilly, who is staring out the window in thought. She is so beautiful, and not in a fake way. Unlike most girls I meet, who wear a lot of makeup, dye their hair, and try their hardest to look perfect, Tilly just looks perfect.

"Ready to go?" I ask, clearing my throat.

"Sure." She snaps out of whatever thought she had and smiles at me as she clears her plate and follows me to my car.

"So? Do you drive?" I ask as I wait for her to put her seatbelt on.

"Yes, but my car is with my family in France," she says with a sigh.

Why would she have left so quickly, and without her car? She only had one suitcase when she turned up here, and it's clear she hasn't planned any of this. Something else is going on.

"You could ask someone in your family to drive it here," I respond, watching her carefully for her reaction. My siren is hiding something, and every lie she tells me is going to help me figure it out. I could ask a friend I know to look her up and I could have every detail of her life sent to me tomorrow, but it feels wrong to do that. I want her to trust me, and it bothers me that I even care this much. She is digging her way into my life without even trying, and I'm just handing her the shovel.

"No, I will just figure it out," she mutters, looking out the window as I drive out of the driveway.

"Well, my old Range Rover is in the garage. It's just a spare so no one will miss it if you want to borrow it," I tell her.

"Really?" she asks, a little taken back.

"Really." I smirk at her as she smiles.

"Thanks. I mean, you don't have to be so, well, nice to me," she says quietly, and I glance over at her.

"I don't, but I know when someone has had a hard time and needs someone to be nice for once," I say, looking away as I drive the rest of the way to work in silence.

I watch Tilly as she looks around the gym when I open all the doors. I can't take my eyes off the way her red hair shines in the morning sun and how little bits of stray hair move with the light wind. The way her bright eyes seem to understand me with one look as she smiles at me. Tilly is something to be stared at, she is so beautiful.

"Here is where you will be and right down that corridor, at the end, is my office." I point it out to her before leading her around the desk.

I quickly show her how to work the computer and show her the diary. I show her how to log people in, as that's the only complicated part.

"If anyone new joins, just call my office and I'll sort them out if you have any issues." She nods at me.

I turn to say hello to some of the early regulars coming into the gym and nearly growl when a guy winks at Tilly, making her smile. Maybe this wasn't a good idea.

"I'm going to my office," I mutter to Tilly, who gives me a small smile before I turn to leave.

# CHAPTER 6
TILLY

"Can you tell Harley I need to see him?" a woman asks as she leans over the counter, smiling at me.

She is older than I am, I would guess she's in her mid-thirties, and she is stunning with light-blond hair and a body that shows she uses the gym a lot. She has a small crop top on, which her large breasts are nearly falling out of, and I bet they would if she attempted to run on a treadmill.

"He said no one other than family is allowed to interrupt him today, sorry," I explain, and she narrows her eyes at me. "I can take a note," I say.

"He will want to see me, don't worry about it," she says and then walks off down the corridor toward Harley's office.

I get up and go to follow her, but I suddenly feel

sick. Instead of walking any further, I open the door to the bathroom near me and run to the nearest toilet. I don't know how long I'm puking before I feel a warm hand rubbing my back and pulling stray bits of hair away from my face.

"Here," I hear Harley say to me before he passes me some tissue, and I wipe my mouth as I stand up.

Harley surprises me by taking my hand and nodding his head toward the bathroom door. He walks us out and straight to his office, opening it for me. I walk in and look around at the massive, wooden desk and the big chair behind it, there is a bookcase and a filing cabinet also in the room. This is an impressive office.

Harley walks over to the mini fridge on top of the filing cabinet after shutting the office door, getting out a bottle of water for me.

"Here." He offers it to me, and I nod, accepting the drink as he pulls out the chair by the desk.

"Please sit, Tilly," he says, and I do, only because I still feel like crap.

Harley sits on the end of the desk, watching me closely, his mind no doubt figuring things out as I drink the water slowly.

"I think–"

"Don't. Please don't say anything you think you know or say it out loud. I just can't–" I mutter, interrupting him. I look down at the ground and stay still as silence fills the room.

"Why are you running, Tilly?" he asks me gently.

"Because I don't want to remember," I answer quietly, lifting my head to meet his gaze.

"I understand that."

"How can you? How can you be so scared of your past that you can't even say the words out loud? That you can't even think about it without shaking or wanting to run," I end up snapping out, and he tilts his head to the side as we stare at each other.

"Because my past keeps me up at night, too," he tells me, shocking me into silence as I see the truth in his eyes.

"Hey, bro," a voice shouts as the office door is slammed open, and I turn to see a man walking in. This must be Sebastian, as he looks so much like Elliot but less wild.

Sebastian has a suit on, his hair is cut short, and his jaw is close shaved. He gives us both a cheeky smile. "And you must be Tilly. Izzy has been telling me about you and your unexpected arrival," he says.

"You're Sebastian, right?" I ask, and he nods.

"The good-looking brother." He points a finger at his chest, making me laugh.

"The brother who has his own office," Harley points out, and Sebastian only grins.

"Was I interrupting something?"

"No, but Tilly isn't feeling well so I'm going to take her home," Harley says.

"I'm fine now," I say, standing up and walking around the desk, but Harley catches my arm, stopping me.

"You sure?" he asks, his thumb rubbing circles on my arm.

It is comforting, and I find myself leaning into him a little. "Certain," I reply, and he lets go after a second's pause. "Nice to meet you, Sebastian," I say as he opens the door for me, nodding.

I walk out of the office and go back to my desk. The rest of the day goes quickly and, before I know it, it's time for us to close up.

"Hey, Tilly, my wife, Maisy, is making dinner and she invited Harley and you to come. She would love to meet you," Sebastian says as he comes out of his office, just as I walk down the corridor toward Harley's office.

"I don't know . . ." I say as I watch Harley come out of his office, locking the door.

"Come on, Maisy makes amazing food, and Jake loves to meet new people," Sebastian says, tilting his head to the side as he looks at Harley and me.

"I guess I can," I say just as Harley gets to us, his eyes locked with mine.

"How are you feeling?" he asks me straight away.

"I'm good now," I tell him.

"Was it just a morning thing?" Harley asks, making my heart pound when I know he is onto what is going on with me. I should just tell him, but I can't seem to make the words come out of my mouth. Let alone, even think the words to say them.

"Yes," I say, giving him the answer he wants without saying another word, and he nods, his eyes moving down my body.

Thankfully, Sebastian starts talking and I can look away from Harley's luring, green eyes when they meet mine. The unspoken word just seems to burn between us.

"Tilly said she is coming to dinner with us. I'm sure you won't disagree with that." Sebastian pats Harley's arm and walks off.

"Meet you two there," Sebastian adds over his shoulder, and neither I nor Harley move.

I don't know what to say to him, or how to say anything. I feel like any chance of him liking me just went flying out the window, and I'm expecting to see a Harley-sized hole in the front door.

"Come on." He sighs after a second of me overthinking everything, shocking me again when he slides his hand into mine as he leads us out of the gym.

"Why are you holding my hand?" I ask him.

"Why are you not letting go?" he responds, and I choose not to answer that as I look away.

I wait for him to lock the doors, and then we get into his car after he unlocks it. The drive out of town is quiet, and I don't feel like saying anything as I just watch him drive. How can someone drive so sexily? Just watching the way he turns the wheel and the way his muscles in his arms flex as he changes gears is beyond hot. I've never noticed that about anyone before, but here I am, staring at a man driving.

I've never had anyone walk into my life and make me feel safe around them, but I feel that way around him. He makes me feel safe, he makes me feel like my past can't haunt me.

We eventually pull into a driveway not far out of town, and a barn conversion house appears at the end. The barn is lit by little solar lights under the windows, and there are two cars parked at the side, which Harley parks next to. I get out my side at the same time as Harley, who seems to just be watching me for something, gets out of his. I almost like that he doesn't demand an answer from me.

"Har-har," is shouted from the door by a wriggling, little boy in the arms of Sebastian.

The little boy has wavy, black hair and a cute, little face. He is dressed in jeans and a white top with a car on it. He is so sweet and loud. How can someone so small be shouting so loud?

"Hey, Jake," Harley says as he picks Jake up from Sebastian, and Jake wraps his little arms around Harley's neck and hugs him. Jake rests his head on his shoulder and looks at me, making me smile, and I stick my tongue out at him, which makes him giggle.

"How old is he?" I ask Sebastian.

"Ten months," he tells me, waving a hand inside the house. "Come in, it's cold out here."

I walk in and slide my heels off as Harley takes his shoes off.

"This way," Sebastian says, and I follow him through the house.

There's a small, cosy-looking lounge and then a dining room before we get to the kitchen, where a girl my age is pulling something out of the oven. She places a tray of what looks like enchiladas down and puts the stove mitts down as she turns to smile at me.

"You must be Tilly," she says, walking over and pulling me into a hug.

I'm a little shocked at her friendly introduction, but I don't mind a hug so I return it. When she leans back, I can't help but think how unfair it is that she has had a baby and is pregnant again and looks amazing. Her long, black hair is up in a messy bun, and she's wearing casual clothes, which show off the tiny, little bump she has.

"I have to say, you look amazing for someone who is pregnant and has a little one already," I say.

"Oh, I don't, but thank you." She laughs as Sebastian wraps an arm around her and kisses the side of her head.

"You're crazy beautiful," he tells her, making her blush a little. "Why don't you two take Jake to the lounge to play with his toys while I help Maisy serve up dinner?" Sebastian says.

"Sounds good," Harley replies, and Jake tightens his hands around Harley's neck as he hugs him again. It's clear Jake loves Harley.

"Here, go and sit with him and I will get some toys out," Harley says and hands me the toddler.

"Err, sure, I mean, yes. I just have never held a little one before."

"You might need the experience one day," he tells me gently as I accept Jake. I manage to place him on my hip, and he reaches up, taking my glasses off and tries to put them into his mouth.

"Nope, these aren't food." I chuckle, and he gives me a toothy grin as I take the glasses from him.

"Har-har," he says, pointing at the door Harley just left through.

"I know, you love Har-har," I say as I hold Jake, and I am surprised by how heavy he is.

I walk over to the rug in the room and sit down with Jake in my lap. Jake tries to crawl away the moment I try to sit him down, and I have to pick him up again. It's only a few minutes of trying to keep his attention before Harley comes in with two trucks in his arms. He puts the trucks in front of Jake, and he crawls over and starts pushing them around the rug.

"Do you like children?" I ask Harley, watching how he looks at Jake.

"Yes, you?" he replies.

"No idea, well, not yet."

"I think you will be a natural," he tells me gently, but he doesn't say anything else as he watches me play with Jake.

*I hope Harley is right.*

## CHAPTER 7
TILLY

"Can I have a word with you before you go to bed?" Harley asks me when we get back from Sebastian and Maisy's house after a lovely meal.

I was surprised by how much information about Harley they managed to tell me over the dinner. I think they both suspect something is going on, so they decided to tell me every good thing they could think of about Harley. I learnt that he always babysits for Jake, and that he helped them so much when Jake was teething and no one was getting any sleep. That Harley's favourite colour is blue, and he likes strawberry cheesecake. They gave me a lot to think about.

I was hoping to avoid any conversation with Harley, so I planned on rushing up the stairs as soon as we got home, but that doesn't seem to be happening. I pause, with my hand on the bannister, and look back at him.

"I'm tired," I respond.

"You can avoid this all you like, but I'm asking you to talk to me. I won't judge you, and I won't stop you from walking away. Anything you tell me, I will never tell anyone else," he tells me gently.

"You will judge me, Harley," I whisper as he moves closer and gently runs his hand down my arm.

"How about I tell you something about me that people judge, and then you can tell me about this?" he asks as he places his hand on my stomach, where there is a slight, hard bump.

"You know anyway."

"Tilly," he says gently, and I nod, knowing that some part of me wants to talk to him, and a bigger part of me already trusts him.

I haven't spoken to anyone about what is going on, and I don't know why, but I kind of trust him. He takes my hand and leads me down to the other set of stairs at the end of the corridor. They lead up to another door, and he opens it before flicking on the light.

The room is a massive, attic conversion, which

has a desk, two sofas, three bookcases, and several old boxes around the room. It's a cosy room and well-used from the looks of the all the things lying around on the desk.

"This is my office, well, office space that I like to be in. I sleep up here some nights," he tells me as he shuts the door behind us, and I walk over to the sofa.

"It's a lovely room," I comment, but he doesn't reply to me.

I sit down, and he comes and sits right next to me, his body pushed against mine. It surprises me when I don't attempt to move.

"How far along are you?" he asks me straight away.

"I thought you were going to tell me something about you first," I say, with a small, awkward laugh.

"Okay . . . fair enough," he says and then clears his throat. "I fight in a place called The Cage, and I have done so since I was a teenager," he says, watching for how I react as he looks down at me.

"Do you win?" I ask. I want to be shocked, but some part of me isn't shocked at all. I knew he had secrets, it's written all over his face. I'm glad it's this, in a way, and not a secret wife and kids he hides in another town or something.

"Every time," he says, but there's a hint of

sadness in his voice which makes me wonder if he likes to win at all.

"Do you hate it?" I ask him, and he runs his hand through his hair, which he left down at Sebastian's when Jake pulled the hairband out.

"Yes," he tells me, and I put my hand on his knee, squeezing gently before I start talking.

"I'm five months pregnant and please don't ask why I don't look pregnant or have much of a bump, it just seems to be that way," I tell him, almost not wanting to tell him this about me. I know most guys would run the other way.

"You can kick me out or run away from me. I get that. I'm a pregnant person you don't know, who moved into your house and kissed you." I mentally cringe as I blurt that out. He looks down at me, shaking his head ever so slightly, but I catch it.

"One time, when I was seventeen, I fought and nearly lost. The fight was bad, and I ended up killing the man to survive. Afterward, I was sitting at the bar and a woman came up to me. She was a lot older than me, and I'd never seen her before, but I will never forget her words."

"What did she say?" I ask him.

"That you fight for the best things in life, you fight to survive, and you don't give up. That anything simple and straightforward isn't going to be worth it. It's the hard things–the complicated things– that challenge you but give you the best rewards. She told me that and then walked away, but the words stuck around. I have a feeling you're one of the best things in life, and I'm not going to walk away." He says each word with emotion, an emotion that I'm feeling too as I feel my heart pounding inside my chest. A silence fills the room as I don't know how to reply to him. We just stare at each other, our faces inches apart.

"I've killed people in my fights, does that not make you want to run from me? Most women would," he asks me gently.

I'm a little shocked by that, but there's something about him that makes me think he wouldn't have done it on purpose. It's just the way he says it, and the way he took Izzy into his home and accepted her as his sister straight away. No questions asked. He looked after her, a heartless killer wouldn't have done that. It's other things too, like the way his family is around him, how they respect him, and it's not out of fear. No, it's respect that is brought on by doing good things and earning it.

"No, it doesn't make me want to run. My family is complicated, but I know that even if someone has been forced to do bad things to survive, it doesn't make them a bad person," I say, thinking of my father for only a second. He was in jail for a year for something he did, but he isn't a bad person. Not one bit of him is.

"Why are you running, Tilly?" he asks. My name is spoken so softly that I almost miss him saying it. I almost want to beg him to whisper my name once more. I keep my eyes locked on his green ones as I answer him.

"I'm running from my ex-boyfriend, the baby's father," I say quietly, watching as he nods, his eyes blazing.

"What did he do?" Harley asks, but even thinking of that night has me tensing up.

Harley notices and pulls me closer to his side, wrapping his arm around my waist. I rest my head on his shoulder. I don't even think I can move away if I wanted to, my body just wants to relax against him. I love how he smells when I am this close, like mint.

"Why do I feel safe with you? Why do I trust you when I couldn't even trust my family to talk to them before I ran?" I mumble to him.

"I don't know why, but I'm glad you came here, Tilly," he tells me.

"Why is that?" I ask.

"You're not ready for that answer yet," he tells me gently as I look up at him. Harley leans down and presses a kiss to my forehead.

"You still didn't answer my question," he reminds me. I know I didn't, but I don't want to ruin this moment between us with my past. Not yet.

"I can't, I'm not ready to talk about it yet. He hurt me, that's all I will say. I will move out if you want. I know you didn't sign up for a pregnant woman with a messed-up past living in your house," I tell him, because I know it's not fair to expect him to have me stay here.

"No, stay," he says quickly, like he doesn't even have to think twice about it.

"Only for a few weeks," I respond.

"Until you're ready to leave. The baby must come first now, Tilly, and it's safe here. You have people here who care about you and will help," he tells me, and I know he is right. "Tell everyone the baby is mine. Your ex isn't coming near you again."

I blink a few times. "You don't have to—"

"We can talk about it more another time. He isn't touching our baby, Tilly." He smiles at me and I sigh. I rest my head back against his chest. Neither of us saying anything as we hold each other for a long time. I can't remember the last time I just sat and cuddled someone. There isn't anything else expected, and I feel safe. I know I won't be forgetting this day anytime soon. I look over at the bookcases in the room and remember the ones downstairs too.

"Do you read a lot?" I ask, and he laughs.

"Every day if I can get my way. I like to garden, too," he tells me.

"Books are kind of my thing, too. When I left France, I had to leave my collection there. I hope to get them back at some point," I tell him.

"Well, you can borrow anything from here if you want," he offers.

"You sure?"

"Yes, go and look." He nudges me, and I slide off the sofa.

I walk around the bookcases and I'm surprised to see so many old books mixed in with new ones that I've read. It's strange to think that he likes the classic romance and thriller books that I do.

"Wow, a first edition Jane Eyre," I say, picking it up and reading the first page.

"Yes, I had to travel to an auction in London and pay an obscene amount of money for that one, but it's worth it. I will travel anywhere to pick up a limited edition or signed copy I want," he tells me, and I bet he did pay a fortune for this one. There aren't that many around, as far as I know.

I slide it back and pick up a book I haven't

read. It has my favourite paranormal creature, dragons, on the cover. I know you shouldn't judge a book by its cover, but sometimes I do. Pretty covers, as well as the blurbs, sell books to me.

"Can I borrow this?" I ask.

"Of course. I will also move the cot and spare child's wardrobe into your room for you. It's only been used for Jake a few times," he tells me.

"I would like that," I say with a small smile.

"You do need to tell Izzy before she finds out. Izzy sees you like family, and I know she would be upset to find out by accident," he reminds me as I walk to the door.

"She is going to kill me for not telling her," I say with a sigh.

"You might find she will understand. Not everything has been easy for her in the last few years. I believe she has things she hasn't told you," he says, and I know she left out a few things.

"Like the fact her brother fights in a place called The Cage?" I ask.

"All her brothers do," he tells me.

"Is that how you have so much money? Is it really worth it?" I ask, not really understanding why he would risk his life for anything. Even money and a house like this.

"I don't do it for money, or for anything I want. I have no choice," he says, looking down at his phone.

Clearly, he doesn't want to talk anymore, and I don't know what to say. I walk away, shutting the attic door behind me.

*Why would he have no choice?*

## CHAPTER 8
### HARLEY

"Harley, I've been looking for you," Blake says as he walks into the attic, Luke following close behind.

I shut my laptop so they don't see the baby store I have open on it. I've ordered a lot of stuff to come tomorrow as a gift to Tilly, making sure it's all boxed up well so I can tell my family I'm having a room redone or something.

I've never bought a girl anything, and here I am, ordering nappies and cot sheets. I don't know if she will be okay with my buying all this stuff for her and the baby, but I want to help her. It can't be easy running from your past and leaving your family behind when you have a baby on the way. I know I didn't get her pregnant, and she isn't my responsibility, but I can't walk away from her. It feels like she is mine, and it has felt that way since I first saw her.

"I could use a distraction," I say with a laugh, walking over to the sofas where Blake sits looking nervous. I share a look with Luke, who only grins.

"Okay, what's going on? Blake, you look like you're about to shit yourself, while Luke looks like he is waiting for you to do just that," I say, and Blake laughs, but it's a nervous one.

"I want to ask Izzy to marry me, and I would like your permission. She never had a father figure in her life, but she has told me on more than one occasion that she sees you like that," he says, and I'm not entirely surprised he is asking me. I know how much he loves my sister.

"You didn't need to ask me, but yes. I'm going to say this once, though. If you hurt her or do anything other than love that girl, I'm going to beat the shit out of you," I say, watching as he nods at me in understanding. There isn't anything I wouldn't do to protect my sister.

"Congrats, man, but what he said," Luke says, and Blake laughs.

"I'd rather hurt myself than ever hurt her, so don't worry," he tells us, and it makes me feel a little better.

"Can't believe you're actually going to be our

brother-in- law. I always saw you as a brother, even before you started dating our sister."

"I felt more like he was a guy who ate our food, lived in our house most of the time, and made sure Seb found his way home when he was drunk," I comment, with a smile to show him I'm joking.

"Oi! I brought food here sometimes, like food my mum cooked for you guys," Blake responds with a fake, hurt expression.

"Oh, yeah. I'm coming to yours for tea tomorrow night," Luke says with a dreamy look as he rubs his stomach. Even I have to admit the food she sends us is impressive.

"Fine, but no hitting on my mum, it's not funny anymore," Blake says, and I can't help but laugh when Luke winks at him.

"Your mum is hot, though. If only I were twenty years older," Luke says, and Blake throws a pillow at him.

"Harley . . . just . . . thank you for bringing her into my life. I was lost until her, and I know I can't really explain it, but I know I have you to thank for bringing her here."

"I didn't bring her here for you. In fact, when we found out you two were together, I wanted to beat the shit out of you," I tell him honestly.

"Understood. If I had a sister, I would be the same way," Blake replies.

"Luckily, you don't. If she looked anything like your mum–" Luke says, and Blake throws another cushion at him to stop that sentence.

"What's the plan? How are you going to ask?" I ask, changing the conversation.

"Well, she loves the beach so I've booked a private boat in a month, and I'm going to ask her while we're on it," he says.

"That's a good plan," I say, knowing Izzy told me about how her mum used to take her to the beach as a child. The fact he knows that shows me he listens to her. That he loves her.

"I had this ring custom made for her. I've been waiting for it for three months now, but I only want the best for her," he says and hands me a small, white box. I open it to see a ring with one large diamond, and at the side of it sits two, tiny blue stones. I think they are sapphires.

"She will love it," I reply, handing the box back to Blake. Luke doesn't ask to see it, so I'm guessing he spoke to Luke before.

"How is Tilly settling in? Izzy is worried about her, and I'm not sure what to say to Izzy," Blake asks.

"It's been a week, but honestly, Tilly will talk to

Izzy when she is ready," I say, leaning back in my seat and trying not to think about Tilly.

I know she still hasn't told anyone about the baby, but she did listen to me when I suggested registering with the local doctors and hospital. I'm hoping she is going to say something to Izzy tomorrow when she goes out shopping with her. There's no way the siren can hide this from everyone forever.

"A week of him following her around like a lost puppy. I've never seen you so hung up on a girl," Luke comments, and I glare at him.

I go to reply when my phone rings, and I pull it out of my jacket to see Arthur's name flashing on the screen.

"What?" I answer, not wanting to talk to him right now, or ever. We have five fights left, that's it now, and then my family will finally be free of him.

"I had an idea," Arthur says, he sounds cold and calculating.

"I'm waiting," I reply, standing up and walking away from Luke and Blake.

"Five fights left now, and I want one of you to fight five guys, one after another," he says, and there's a moment of silence as I pause in shock. He has to be fucking kidding.

"That's fucking crazy. There is no way any of us could win that," I shout, and he laughs.

"I'm done with you King brothers, and I want this over. I will set up the fight and text you the details. I expect you to be there, Harley, or maybe that pretty, red-headed roommate of yours might go missing," he tells me, and then the line goes dead.

"For fuck's sake," I say, throwing the phone across the room and watching as it smashes into pieces across the floor.

"What happened?" Luke asks, coming over, and I run my fingers through my hair and mentally groan as I look at Luke. I don't want to tell him anything, but I know I won't be able to hide this from my brothers.

"Arthur has decided to do the last five fights one after another. And only one of us can fight them all," I say, and Luke shakes his head. He knows the chances of any of us surviving that are low, or impossible. It only takes one of them to hit too hard, or another to bring a weapon in, to change the odds.

"Fuck, no," Luke says as Blake comes over.

"He's setting you up to fail, it'll be suicide walking into that fight!" Blake comments, hearing the conversation.

"I don't have a choice. I'm the only one with any hope in hell to finish this," I say, sighing.

I would never let any of my brothers do this for me. I would never let them die because of our father's mistakes. The fact he threatened Tilly is another matter entirely.

"You've always protected us, Harley. We aren't going to let you fight this and die to protect us," Luke says, grabbing my arm.

"It's my choice," I tell him, pulling away.

Except, it really isn't my choice, and when I think about Tilly, I know I can't be with her now. Not like I want to be. It will break her heart if I don't walk out of that cage, and I can't do that to her. I already like her too much to hurt her. For a second, I thought I had my happy ending; the girl I want and a future with a child that isn't mine, and I would do anything to help bring the baby up. I can't even have children myself, not after one of my past fights destroyed my chances to have children in one attack. That's why I help with Jake as much as possible because I know I'll never have that chance to hold a baby. But with Tilly, I could have been there for her and her child. Now, being there can only hurt her more.

I walk out of the office and down the two flights of stairs and into the garden. I open the greenhouse up after walking across to it and pulling out a shovel. I need to dig up the old soil by the tree and put some new soil down before planting the flowers. I shove a bag of soil into the wheelbarrow and add the shovel before pushing it out of the greenhouse.

Digging the shovel into the ground, I get to work. The clouds above are dark, and it almost looks like it may rain later. I don't let it disturb me, though, because this is a distraction I need right now. I like gardening because it takes my mind off of everything, and I can just work. I have most the soil dug up by the time the first bit of rain falls, and I shove my stuff back into the greenhouse just as the heavens open up and it begins to pour down.

I am making my way back across the garden when I see Tilly looking at me from the window. She smiles gently at me, her eyes drifting over my soaking wet top and how my hair is down. I don't think she has seen me like this before. Tilly and I just stare at each other before I get to the back door and I'm forced to look away. I wonder if she feels like I do, how all I want to do is walk into that kitchen and kiss her, screw the consequences.

## CHAPTER 9
### TILLY

"That one is cute," Izzy says as she points to a red top that's on sale.

I love it, but I know it's pointless to buy anything when I'm only going to get bigger. My bump seems to have grown in the last two weeks, and now, it's no longer easy for me to wear tight dresses or tops.

I saw the doctor and a midwife yesterday, who checked the baby's heartbeat and booked me in for a scan. They think everything is going well and that I'm just one of those lucky women whose pregnancy bump doesn't show. In some ways, I'm glad I didn't show until now. For two days, Harley has avoided me, making small talk and pretending the moments we had together didn't happen. I don't know how we went from cuddling on the sofa to small talk over dinner. It's gotten to the point where he walks out the door when I walk into a room sometimes. I'm so confused by him. I look at my friend, knowing I've been avoiding her, myself, for the last week.

"We need to talk," I tell Izzy, who stops moving tops across a rack. I nod my head in the direction leading out of the store and go to sit by the fountain outside. I sit down on a bench, and Izzy sits next to me.

"Come on then, I'm worried," she says, nudging my shoulder a little, and I take a deep breath.

"I'm pregnant," I tell her quietly. She doesn't move as she stares at me. Izzy pulls me into a tight hug after a long pause between us, and I wrap my arms around her. We don't say anything for a while, just holding each other, and I'm sure she is working a few things out in her head.

"I'm happy for you, but I know there is more to this story. How far gone are you?" she asks me, guessing straight away there's a reason I'm scared to have this baby.

Izzy has been asking questions every time I've seen her for the last two weeks, but I've just avoided them, wanting to try to figure out how to tell her. To be strong enough to. I've never thought of myself as a weak person, but the idea of telling anyone my most vulnerable moment terrifies me. The idea of sharing that part of myself is scary.

"I'm five months," I tell her.

"Wow . . . you look good. I'm kind of jealous, and I'm sure Maisy will be, too. She is huge and she's only four months." She laughs, pulling my hands to her and holding them.

"Wait . . . maybe don't tell her that. Not like huge in a bad way, just in a pregnant way, you know?" she says, and I laugh with a nod. "In fact, I'm just mumbling because I'm in shock, and this wasn't what I expected you to say," she finishes.

"What did you expect?" I ask.

"Erm . . . maybe something about you and Harley?" she asks, and I shake my head, not wanting to approach that subject. Thankfully, she asks another question after an awkward silence between us. "Does your family know?"

"No, I left before I could tell them. Part of me didn't want to because I knew they would never let me leave," I tell her.

"Why did you leave? I know your parents would have supported you, and your brothers would have too," she says, and I know she is right. My family would have helped me, but I couldn't risk them not believing me. I couldn't risk them believing me, either, and having my dad, or brothers, attacking Daniel.

"The father. Well, he–" I go to say, and my voice cracks. Even now, I don't know how to tell her. Even after preparing it in my head for so long.

"Were you with him long? Does he know?" she asks me.

"We were together seven months, and no, I never told him about the baby," I tell her. I hope he never finds out.

"Are you planning on telling him?" she asks me gently.

"Trust me, if I had my way, he'd never find out, or go near me again," I say, my words firm.

"You ran from him," she says gently, and I nod, leaning back on the bench and looking up at the clouds. It's a nice day, but it looks like there will be rain later.

"I met Daniel at a party in France and we instantly liked each other. He was hot, smart, and funny. What's not to like, right?" I laugh a little. "So, we started dating, and he got close with my brothers. My whole family loved him like another child. Daniel is a little older than me, and Devon became best friends with him practically overnight because

Devon looked up to Daniel, in a way. The next thing I knew, Devon had invited Daniel to move into our house, and somehow my parents were okay with this," I say.

"That was how long into your relationship?" Izzy asks gently.

"About a month," I say, and she nods, squeezing my hand, so I continue.

"At first, he was lovely and stayed in the spare room. Then after a week, he moved his stuff into my room, and I just let him. He has this way of sweet talking you into anything, I can't explain it, but my family loved him. I guess I thought I did, too. Then everything changed."

"How?" she asks.

"The first time was at a party. I was dancing with a few girls when a strange man got too close and tried to dance with me. I pushed him away straight away, but Daniel saw and went crazy. I had to listen to him shout at me the whole way home about how I wanted to cheat on him and a load of stuff I wouldn't ever do. When I tried to get out of the car, after he parked outside our house, he grabbed my arm and wrapped his hand around my throat, telling me never to do that again. I had bruises and was terrified of him," I admit. "Still, I let him take me into the house and sleep next to me in my bed like nothing happened. I lay there all night, just shaking, not saying a word."

"Oh, Tilly," Izzy says, squeezing my hand once more, but I continue speaking because I need to say this.

"The next morning, he said he was sorry and charmed my family into thinking some random guy gave me the bruises at a party," I mutter, still annoyed with myself for not saying something. I should have then, but I didn't.

"Why didn't you just leave?" she asks me.

"I planned to, then things just got worse. After the party, he was only nice sometimes, sex became something he demanded, and I got to the point of just doing it to make him happy. We used protection every time, so the baby wasn't planned," I say, knowing how badly that plan went.

"Tell me if you want to, and if you don't . . . well, I'm just glad you're here," she tells me.

"I booked my tickets here and planned everything for a month, and in that month, I found out I was pregnant, which only made me more confident I had to get away. I knew my family had a holiday planned for a week, so that's the only time I could get away from them. I tried to distract Daniel that night by getting him to see his mum. Only, he came back as I was leaving with my suitcase," I say, a tremor in my voice.

"What happened?" Izzy encourages me gently.

"Let's just say I was lucky to escape, Iz. I don't want to talk about it anymore," I whisper, and she nods.

"If it helps, I believe you were right to run. A man like that would never be a good father. Not if he doesn't respect the baby's mother."

"I was scared he would hurt me again, that he would hurt the baby. Daniel is not right," I shake my head, wiping a few tears away.

In some ways, it feels good to get some of the secrets off my chest and have her understand why I won't let Daniel near my baby. I know I will have to tell my baby about their father. Eventually. It's not something I want to hide from him or her.

"Does anyone else know about the baby?" she asks, thankfully changing the subject a little.

"Harley guessed," I say.

"Is he still okay with you living there? I'm sure he would be, but if he isn't, then we will figure something out," she says, and I squeeze her hand.

"He is okay with it. He actually moved Jake's old cot into my room and has been making me breakfast, making sure I eat in the day. He has been looking after me," I say, thinking of him.

My mind wanders back to seeing him in the garden. He was walking in the pouring rain, rainwater dripping all over his body and making his top stick to him, showing off his muscular chest. His hair was down, shaping his stern, handsome face and his bright-green eyes seemed to speak to me. They seemed to call me to him, begging me to run out into the rain and press my lips to his once again. Then he ignored me. So, clearly, he wasn't thinking the same thing as my hormonal brain was thinking.

"Harley is a lot of things, but one of his best qualities is how protective he is. My brothers look after their own, and they know how you helped me when I lost Mum. How you're like a sister to me, and I'm damn well going to be there for you now," she tells me, wiping her own tears away. I look her over, remembering being there when she watched her mum die and begging my parents not to move away. My parents had no choice, and I never told Izzy of the problems my family had, but I know my mum never wanted to leave her.

"I love you, Iz, you know that? I'm always going to be here for you, too," I tell her, and she laughs, wiping more tears away before pulling me into a hug.

"Good, because there's no way you're getting rid of me," she whispers.

"Izzy!" I hear a voice shout, and we pull away from the hug to see a blond woman walking over. She has golden-blond hair with brown tips, and she is gorgeous as she bounces over. She's wearing a leather jacket, a white top, and black skinny jeans.

"Allie," Izzy says, standing up and pulling Allie into a hug when she gets near.

"This is Tilly, and, Tilly, this is Allie," Izzy introduces us as I stand up, and I hold a hand out to Allie, who knocks it away and pulls me into a hug.

"None of that. I feel like we are friends anyway with how much Izzy has told me about you," she tells me as she lets go.

"Nice to meet you, Allie. I've heard lovely things about you from Izzy," I tell her, and she grins.

"I've heard from Luke that you and Harley have been sharing sexy looks for weeks. So . . . you fancy the oldest King brother?" Allie asks, making me a little speechless.

"Err . . ." I say.

"It's okay. The King brothers are the hottest men for miles. And you're living with one. I'm dating one, so I get it," she tells me with a cheeky look that makes me laugh.

"These are my brothers . . ." Izzy groans, and I laugh a little with Allie.

"Damn, I wanted to tell you all about this thing Elliot did last night, and I swear I–" Allie starts saying.

"Lalalala . . ." Izzy interrupts, and Allie winks at me.

"I'll text you it later, Tills," she says, and I laugh.

When Izzy told me about Allie, she did say she is really honest. Clearly about everything, but something tells me I'm going to like her.

"I wish I could stay and catch up, but I'm in a rush to get to Tristan's. He annoyed the nurse the other day and she won't come back, so until he gets both the casts off next week, I'm looking after him," Allie tells us both.

"What did he say to the nurse? Tria was lovely, and I thought they were really getting along. I mean, Luke told me Tristian had actually been getting out of bed and trying," Izzy comments.

"Urgh, I don't know. Tris is a mess at the moment after everything that happened, and I doubt he meant whatever he said to Tria," she says, and Izzy nods, a silence spreading between us all.

*What happened?* I wonder.

"He will be all right, but I will speak to my

brothers and Blake and see if they can go over to cheer him up a little," Izzy offers.

"Elliot's been trying, but yeah, that may help," she says, and Izzy nods, hugging her once more.

"I will see you on the weekend, okay?" Allie asks.

"Definitely. I need to tell you about this secret trip Blake has planned for us. He seems really nervous about it," Izzy says with a frown.

"Ooh, I wonder what it is," I comment.

"Me, too," Allie replies, and her phone starts ringing in her pocket.

"Damn it, I need to go, but love ya both and see you soon," she says, walking off and pulling her phone out of her jacket.

"Anything else you want to tell me before we go and shop for some maternity clothes? No wonder you didn't want to buy any clothes from the other stores," Izzy comments.

"Not me, but I want you to explain the fighting, The Cage, and what the hell happened to your brothers," I say, and she nods with a sigh, waving a hand toward the bench.

"This is going to be a long story," she begins.

I sit down as she explains about Arthur and her father. She tells me how her brothers are fighting to pay off a debt, and how they're close to being free. She tells me everything that's happened since she moved here, and what has recently happened to Tristan. By the time we leave our spot on the bench, I feel sorry for Harley, everything he's been through, and how he's always been the one to protect them all. He's a good man, and I hope when he and his brothers are free of this debt he can live a healthy life.

Only, I want to be in that life, too.

## CHAPTER 10
### HARLEY

"What the hell do you want?" I ask as I walk into my father's room after he called me to tell me it's urgent. I stop in my tracks when I see Hazel, my ex-girlfriend and the only girl I've ever cared about, in bed with my father. They are kissing, ignoring me completely, and when my father moves away, she sees me and covers her naked body with a sheet.

"What the fuck, Hazel?" I ask her, and she nervously looks at my father and me.

"This is my new girlfriend, and she is moving in here," Father says.

I walk out of the room, ignoring the pain shooting through my chest. I expected it from him, but not her. Not the first girl I've ever slept with, the first girl I actually cared about. I run down the stairs and out of the house, *and I just keep running through the trees, having no idea where I'm going. I trip on a rock and slam onto the ground just as it starts raining. Half of me wants to stand up and keep running, but the other half of me knows I can't do that. I can't take my brothers with me, I would never get custody at seventeen. I lift myself up off the ground and tighten my jaw as I look up at the dark clouds.*

*Only a few more years and we can all leave this shithole of a town, and our heartless father with it.*

"Hey, what are you doing in here?" Tilly asks me, snapping me from my memories of a night I'd rather forget.

Hazel was my father's girlfriend until he was killed, and she never left me alone the entire time. She played on my feelings, making me hate women until recently. Until Tilly, who understands me with one look. She doesn't push me, she doesn't hurt me.

I turn around and see her standing at the entrance to her bedroom. She walks in and places her laptop on the bed; she must have been working all day editing a new book she was sent last night. Tilly looks way too beautiful today, she seems even more stunning every day, and it's so difficult to stay away from her. Not to kiss her, to take off the tight clothes she has on, which show off her amazing body. Not to finally run my fingers through her soft hair.

"The roses in the garden needed cutting, I

thought you might like some," I say, moving to the side so she can see the massive vase full of at least twenty red roses. I hate cutting them, but sometimes you have to cut the beauty away from something to let it bloom.

"Oh, Harley, they are stunning," she says, coming over and touching the flowers' petals. I look down at her and, at the same time, she stares up at me, an awkward silence between us.

"They aren't the only thing in the room that is stunning," I say, and she laughs.

"You have a high opinion of yourself, Harley King," she says, moving away as I laugh.

"That could have been a romantic moment between us, and there you go . . ." I say, both of us still laughing.

"Damn, totally ruined it." She chuckles.

I go to sit down next to her on the bed and move a book I find. It's a children's fairy tale, The Princess and the Pea.

"It was my favourite growing up. I used to get scared my dad would go back to prison and I would wake up crying, and my mum always read this book to me. It was the only story I would fall asleep to," she tells me. I didn't know her dad went to jail.

"Why did your dad go to jail? If you don't mind me asking?" I ask her.

She sits and crosses her legs, her little bump showing through her tight, white top. "My dad wasn't always a good guy. He is now, but as much as my mum tried to hide his past from us as children, it didn't work. Can you remember that as I tell you everything?" she asks gently, and I nod.

"He was one of the five leaders of a major drug and illegal weapons company. Basically, they moved things from Africa, and other countries, into Europe. My dad told me his father and his grandfather ran the business before him and he was born into it. That's not an excuse, but it's hard to escape what you're born into."

"If anyone understands that, it's me," I say quietly. "What changed?"

"My mum; he met my mum, and she gave him a choice. Her or his work," she says, her voice quiet.

"And he chose her?" I respond.

"Yes, he did. He only served a year because he gave evidence in the trials of all of his business partners and told the police where to find everything. Then he and my mother were given a new identity and last name," she explains.

I guess it makes some sense, the police would have done anything for the information her father gave them, and then the new identity as a reward.

"Fox?" I say, and she nods.

"And then they started having kids and lived happily ever after." She chuckles, but it's almost sad.

"Does he ever speak about his old life? Did he easily manage to move on?" I ask, knowing my own past haunts me. I don't think I will ever be able to put The Cage behind me, or what our father did, and manage to sleep at night without my nightmares haunting me.

"He did, with my mum at his side. He says that she chases away his darkness," she tells me, and I know she means more than just her dad now, as she stares back at me. Her blue eyes seem to search my face for a long time, looking for something I don't know how to give her. Feelings I've stopped myself from having since Hazel, but I can't stop the way I look back at her. I can't stop how I feel for her, the siren is working her way into my heart whether I like it or not.

"Maybe some darkness can't be kept away."

"All darkness can be kept away, you just need to find your light," she says, standing up and leaning over to kiss me on the cheek.

I watch as she walks out of the room, leaving the door open, and I watch, wondering if Tilly could be that light for me. I wonder if she could be the one to stop the darkness of my past from haunting me.

# CHAPTER 11

TILLY

"Thank you for all of this," I whisper to Izzy as she walks us into her apartment, which has been done up for the baby shower she's throwing Maisy and me.

Seconds later, everyone jumps up from where they were hidden and shouts surprise. I want to say it's a surprise, but I overheard her telling Harley something the other day, so I knew. I laugh and smile as someone switches the lights on, and I get a look at the room.

There are pink and blue decorations everywhere, with flowers and balloons spread around the room. I don't know all the women here, but most look familiar, and I've possibly seen them around the gym. There's a counter full of presents, in two large piles, and I know I will have to send 'thank you' letters to everyone for the gifts. They don't really know me that well, and yet, they clearly bought me baby gifts. I try not to feel the pang of sadness I do when I realise my mother isn't here, not that I expected her to be. I just never imagined having a baby shower without her.

"It's nothing." Izzy waves a hand at me, motioning me inside as she speaks.

"You look lovely," Allie says as she walks up to me with Maisy at her side. I give her a hug, looking at the weird pink and blue bows clipped to her blue dress. Maisy tries to hug me, but both our large bumps get in the way.

"Aha, even though I'm a month behind you, my bump is huge," Maisy comments, and it's true. Her bump is massive on her small frame, whereas mine is still small. I remember the baby scan that Harley came with me to, how they said the baby is curled up around my spine and it's normal.

"I think it's because Tilly is taller than all of us," Allie says, and she might be on to something.

"Okay, what is with all the bows?" I ask her, seeing that all the women have them on and Maisy doesn't.

"Okay, so it's game. Everyone got a bow when they came in, and if you say 'baby' then you have to give your bow, or bows, to whoever you were talking to. Whoever has the most at the end gets a prize," she says, clipping a bow onto my red maternity dress. I smooth it down and look at my red dress, seeing my little bump.

"How come you don't have one?" I ask Maisy, who laughs before answering.

"I gave up when I walked in. I can't not say baby, and the prize is useless for us pregnant people." She winks, so I'm guessing it's alcoholic.

"Congratulations on the baby coming, I'm Emilia," a woman with curly, brown hair says, coming over. She's wearing a black hoodie and black jeans, which is different from the room full of women in dresses, but it doesn't take away from her beauty. She has tanned skin and big, brown eyes.

"Hi, I'm Tilly, nice to meet you," I say, shaking her hand.

"I live with Izzy and Blake here," she tells me, and it makes some sense. "But I'm off, I just wanted to say hello."

"You could stay, it looks like there is plenty to drink and eat," I say, noticing the massive buffet table in the lounge, which is full of baby-themed food. There is even a cake shaped like a cradle, with 'Baby Fox' written in icing on the side.

"Thanks, but my dad called, and yeah, I have to

go. We should hang out another time, though." She smiles, and I nod.

"Bye, Em." Allie gives her a hug before she waves to everyone else and leaves.

"We have games planned." Allie winks, taking my hand and leading me over to some women who are standing around.

We chat for a bit with some of the women, who do remember me from the gym, and the others seem nice when we are introduced. I spend the next hour eating and talking to the women here, most give me horror stories about their births, and others offer advice that may be useful to know when the baby comes. Overall, it's fun, and the food is amazing.

"Okay, the painter is here," Izzy says as she comes over to me, with a woman at her side. The woman is older with a huge bag hanging from her shoulder.

"This is a gift from us to both you and Maisy," Izzy whispers.

"Hi, I'm Daisy, and I paint pictures on your bump. It's called Bump art. I have a portfolio you can look through and choose from, but I can do anything you want," the woman says, and I can't help the smile I give them all as they wait for me and Maisy to say something. It's actually really sweet.

"I'm also a photographer, so I will take some

photos that you can keep," she says, and I can't help but think it's the perfect gift.

"You can go first," I whisper to Maisy, who gives me an excited look before following Daisy and Allie into a bedroom, some of the women following.

I go over and choose some food from the massive collection, and I'm halfway through eating a fantastic cupcake when Harley, Sebastian, and Elliot walk in. Harley comes straight over to me, and I can't take my eyes off him as he does.

"I thought guys weren't invited?" I ask, and he smirks as he sits next to me. I watch as he dips his finger into the icing on the cupcake and sucks it off his finger.

"I've never played by the rules, siren." He chuckles, knowing precisely what he is doing.

"Neither have I," I whisper back, dropping my tone just as Maisy comes out of the bedroom with her bump on show. There is an amazing painting of a moon with a stork flying across it, and there is a purple-sky as background with flowers at the bottom of her bump.

"Wow," I hear Sebastian say, and he comes over, trying to place his hand on the bump, but Maisy moves away.

"It's not dry yet," she says with a laugh, and he leans over, kissing her cheek.

"Don't you want a relationship like that?" I ask Harley.

"I don't do relationships. I don't date. I would only hurt someone if I tried," he says, clearly meaning me, and I have to look away from him.

"Tilly, it's your turn. Your boyfriend can come with you if you want?" she asks, looking at Harley and me.

"Oh, he isn't my boyfriend. Harley doesn't do relationships," I say, and Harley glares at me as I stand up and walk off with Daisy.

"For someone that doesn't do relationships, the way he just looked at you was awfully possessive," Daisy comments.

I look back at Harley, who is still staring at me, his eyes are passionate and a tight smile sits on his lips. Possessive is definitely a word I would use to describe the look he is giving me, but it makes no difference. Harley King says he doesn't play by the rules, but he won't break his own rule for me.

## CHAPTER 12

TILLY

"This dress is not going to work now," I comment, looking down at the dress I'm currently trying to pull over my bump. It doesn't fit anymore, not like it did just last week, and I groan. I went from having a small bump to a massive one in over a week.

There are a few knocks at the door as I pull the dress off. I put it back on a hanger in the wardrobe, and I shout, "One second!"

I pull my jeans and long jumper on. Thankfully, it falls to my knees but still shows off my big bump. After I quickly pull my hair out of my jumper and make sure I look okay, I pull the door open to see Harley leaning against the wall, and he smiles at me.

"I want to take you out tonight," he says, and I lean my head to the side. This was not what I expected when I opened the door. Harley has all but glared at me since the baby shower two days ago, when I said he doesn't do relationships. But it wasn't like I was lying. I don't get what he wants from me. It's like he is hot and cold with me all the time, but I don't know what the reason is.

"Where?" I ask him.

"Somewhere nice, you need to get out. This last week, you've been inside so much since you took maternity leave from the gym," he reminds me, and I know he is right.

I took my maternity leave earlier than I thought I would to get finished with my editing work. Harley doesn't seem to mind me not working, but he apparently doesn't like me staying out of his way all week.

"Okay . . . but where?" I ask, and he smirks.

"It's a surprise. I can't tell you, but I know you will like it," he says, flirting with me a little, and some part of me wants to tell him to stop messing with me. To tell me if he wants to be with me or not. But another part of me knows he is messed-up from his past, and maybe he just needs time. That same part of me knows what I'm feeling for him is moving beyond a simple crush, and it's hurting my heart.

"Come on, then." I laugh and, trusting him not to lead me anywhere strange, walk down the stairs.

Luke is at the bottom. Clearly, he has been working

out or something, as he is dripping with sweat as he passes us on the stairs in just some shorts. Damn, he has an eight pack, and I find myself having to pull my eyes away. These Kings are way too hot for their own good. Harley glares at Luke, and I'm not sure why.

"Date?" he asks us both and then smirks when Harley wraps an arm around my waist. "Doesn't matter, you won't tell me anyway," he says, walking slowly up the stairs.

"Yes, it is a date," Harley answers, and I give him a strange look.

"About time." Luke laughs and walks up the stairs.

"Thought you couldn't date me?" I ask Harley as he keeps his arm around me while we walk over to where the coats and shoes are hanging.

"No . . . I can't be with you and not hurt you. This is just my way of dealing with things, but it doesn't change how I want you. I'm not going to avoid that," he tells me.

"It's a crappy way not to be with me. Especially when you look at me the way you do and then want to take me on a date. You're a confusing man, and most people would just think you're stringing me along," I say, and he groans, rubbing his face. I just shake my head at him. "I didn't say no to the date, maybe I'm just a fool for you." I laugh as I pull my coat on and my boots.

"You're no fool, Tilly," Harley says gently as he grabs his coat and keys before leading us outside. When we make it to his car, he opens the passenger door for me. When we get inside, he drives us out of town and down some country roads before we get to the place he pulls into. It's an aquarium, and it's closed as its eight p.m., but the lights are still on inside.

"I hope you like fish and turtles. My friends run this place and left me with the keys for the night. I thought you might like to have a look around when no one is here," he says, and I smile at him.

"It's perfect, thank you," I say, letting myself out of the car before he replies.

It's an unusual date, but it is cute of him. He gets out and goes to the backseat, pulling out a backpack as I wait for him before he takes my hand and leads us inside after opening the door.

"What's in the bag?" I ask him.

"Dinner, seeing as you didn't come down for it today, I packed up some food for us both instead," he says, and I kind of love that he noticed I didn't eat. That he thought of me.

"Good idea," I mutter, my cheeks a shade of red

that probably matches my hair as we walk silently down an aisle of fish.

There are so many different types, but my favourite are the seahorses, and maybe the colourful mixed fish I can't remember the name of. The place is beautiful, and I love how quiet it is. Usually, when you go to places like this, it's so busy that you can't enjoy the animals around you.

"Here, this tunnel is really cool. I used to bring my brothers here sometimes to get them out of the house and distracted. They would spend hours in here," Harley says, opening a door to an underwater tunnel.

There are sharks and turtles and all sorts of fish swimming over the lit-up tunnel, and I stop in the middle of it as Harley opens his bag. He pulls out a blanket, placing all of the food and drinks he brought on the blanket.

"Picnic in an underwater tube. I have to give it to you, Harley, this is amazing and unique," I say, and he holds a hand out, helping me to sit before he sits himself.

"I don't want you to forget our first date," he says with a smirk, and I shake my head at him.

Harley King is confusing. We eat the food he has made before he puts it all away and lies down on the blanket. I lie down on his shoulder and look up at the sharks, who seem to look at us as they swim by.

"Did your brothers like coming here?" I ask him.

"Yes. They loved whenever I would take them out of the house and away from my father. I tried my best to do that, but it was impossible to do it all the time," he says, and all I can think of is the responsibility he must have had as a teenager. He must have had a complicated and stressful youth.

"I bet it was. Izzy told me about your father, about everything," I tell him gently, noticing how he tenses a little, but I slide my hand into his and rest our joined hands on his stomach.

"And you still haven't run from me?" he asks, his words seeming to echo around the tube.

"Why would I?" I reply.

"I'm messed-up, too messed-up for someone like you." He sighs.

"What's that meant to mean?" I ask him, and he lets go of my hand and turns to face me. He lifts some of my long hair and lets it fall through his fingers.

"I can't give you anything, not really. I spent my life protecting my brothers and then Izzy. Even when all the fights with The Cage are over, I will always be looking over my shoulder, expecting Arthur to try something. I will always have to be careful. What kind of life is that for you? For your child?" he asks me, and it starts to make sense to me now.

"You will always protect them, right?" I ask him, and he nods.

"What about you? Don't you want your own family?" I ask him.

"Yes, of course I do, but I won't be able to have that anyway," he says, and I'm confused by his answer. I don't know what he means.

"Explain that to me? I don't get it," I ask him.

"I can't have children, I can't give you a family, and I can't be what you need. All right?" he says in a sharp voice, sitting up and looking away from me.

"I'm sorry, Harley, but it doesn't matter to me," I say gently.

"It will eventually matter when you want us to have a child, and I can never give you that. The fighting came with a cost for me, and the cost was too high," he says. Every part of his body is tense as he stares at the floor.

"Harley," I say, resting my head on his shoulder after sitting up.

"The fighting wasn't the only thing my father made me do, he made me fuck whoever he wanted me to. He made it so I ended up never trusting women, never wanting to get close to anyone." He pauses, taking a long breath. "I never wanted to get hurt again, and then you came into my life. The first woman I couldn't stop thinking about, wanting to be around all the time. But I'm not stupid, I know you won't want a messed-up man," he tells me, looking down at the floor like it holds all the answers in the world.

"You're not messed-up, and it's up to me what I want," I whisper.

He doesn't move for a long time, both of us staring at the fish around us until he looks down at me. The emotion in his eyes is hard to look away from; the hurt he feels, the doubt flashing behind his eyes. I lean up and kiss him, not caring about what he thinks and what he believes is right. I know what I feel for him, and I want him to know. I push all of my feelings for Harley into the kiss, all my worries and everything I know about him.

"Tilly." He sighs when I crawl over and sit on his lap, but he doesn't stop kissing me back. His lips battle with my own as he loses whatever control he was holding on to. The kissing is finished when the baby kicks, and I know Harley felt it as he looks down to where my bump is touching his stomach.

"Can I?" he asks me, and I nod. Harley reaches a hand between us and smooths a hand over the bump. The baby kicks, and he smiles.

"I will be there for you both, I just can't make you any promises until the final fight is done. I don't want to hurt you," he tells me, and I understand, in a way, that this is his way of keeping some control over his life. Unlike when his life was controlled by his father for all those years.

"No promises." I sigh, and he kisses my forehead. I understand where he is coming from, but it doesn't mean I'm giving up on Harley King.

# CHAPTER 13
## HARLEY

"Another King win!" my father shouts, holding my hand by the arm as I glare at him. Not that he gives a crap. I look down at the guy on the floor, blood covering most of his face, his nose is broken, and only the movement of his chest tells me he is even alive anymore. I tried not to hurt him too much, but the man wouldn't give up. He fought like everything in his life depended on it, and I bet it did.

"Get off," I growl, pulling my arm away and walking out of the cage and slamming the door open to the changing room. I hear his booted footsteps as he follows me in here, but I don't turn to him.

"I want to tell you something. I have a plan," he says.

"What?" I snap, looking over my shoulder at him, and he shakes his head.

My father looks every bit the rough man I know he is,

*with his bald head, tattooed neck, and pristine suit. Most people are scared of him with just one look, but no one realises just how evil he really is. Evil with a good-looking face.*

*"Not here," he says, and I ignore him as I get dressed and wipe the blood off my hands. My lip feels like it needs stitches as it continues to bleed, and two of my knuckles feel broken as I undo the bindings.* Fucking great.

*I won't show him that I'm in pain, show him any weakness. I follow my father out of the changing room, seeing him nod to Arthur, who is sitting at the bar, and then he leads me outside. I don't say a word as he drives us back to the house. Not a word, and that's concerning. Fuck knows what crazy plan he has now.*

*"Wait," my father says as I try to walk straight up the stairs and to my room.*

*I glance back at him, watching as he walks into the kitchen. I follow him and see all my brothers sitting around, some are eating and I assume they were talking before Dad came in. They always stop talking when he is here, always scared of his reaction and not wanting a beating. I hate that that's how they have become.*

*"I'm going to kill Arthur and take over The Cage and the other businesses," my father says, and I just stare at him.*

*"You're mad," Elliot growls out, and I give him a look that makes him look away. Elliot is the only one who chal-*

*lenges him these days. Sebastian spends as much time as he can away from the house, and Elliot covers for him. I protect them all, especially Luke. He is the most shielded from everything.*

*"No, I'm not. It's all planned, and when I'm the boss, not just a fucking partner, you can all work for me. It's a brilliant plan. I'm going to sleep and think about it," he says, walking out of the room, and we all sit in silence for a long time. I know my father has mental issues, I've always known that, but this just proves he is fucking crazy.*

*"Should we stop him?"*

*"No," I say quietly, almost hoping Arthur figures out what's going to happen and kills my father. It would be doing us all a favour, and the silence from my brothers suggests they feel the same way.*

I shoot up in bed, the sound of someone screaming fills my ears and makes the memory wash away. That night was the start of my father getting himself killed and ultimately screwing us over. I should have stopped him, waited until Luke turned eighteen, and then we all could have run. Instead, our father getting himself killed just made our lives worse.

I get out of bed quickly and run across the room and open my door, hearing that it's Tilly screaming. I open her door and run into the room, seeing her thrashing around on her bed, the sheets sticking to her as she screams.

"Don't do this, please don't, Daniel," she shouts, and I go over, shaking her shoulder and watching as she suddenly wakes up and jumps.

"Hey, it's me. It's Harley," I say, rubbing a hand down her arm. The moonlight shines through the window and bounces off her pale eyes as she watches me. She looks so scared.

"What . . . what are you doing in here?" she asks me, her voice breathless and scared.

"You were having a bad dream and screaming. I didn't know what was going on and you seemed so scared. I had to wake you up," I tell her.

"Oh, I'm sorry I woke you," she says, rubbing a hand over her pale face and brushing the hair from her eyes.

I hand her the glass of water from the side as I turn the lamp on that's on her desk. She drinks some of the water before handing me the cup.

"Don't be sorry, you're not the only one who has bad dreams, siren," I say, and she nods, understanding clouding her face.

"Want to talk about it?" I ask her after a moment's silence.

"Maybe? I don't know. Does it help you to talk

about it?" she asks me, rubbing a hand over her stomach.

"I don't know. I don't talk about my past to anyone," I tell her. The most I've spoken about my past is to Tilly.

"You should. I mean, you could talk to me. I'm your friend," she says. I don't want to haunt her with my past, and re-living it never seems to help me.

"Have you felt any kicks?" I ask her, changing the subject, and she nods.

"He or she kicks all the time," she tells me. I lift a hand and place it on her stomach, listening as her breath hitches, and I look up to meet her eyes. I don't feel the baby move, but I keep my hand still on her stomach, hoping I do.

"Will you tell me about what happened with your ex, with Daniel? I want to know everything I can about you, and I don't know why," I ask her.

"How do you know his name?" she asks as I move onto the bed and stretch myself out next to her.

"You sleep talk," I answer, staying still as she lies down on the bed and rests her head back on her pillows. We both lie facing each other, neither one of us wanting to say anything.

"Daniel is the baby's father and my ex-boyfriend, who I lived with," she tells me.

"Why isn't he here?" I ask her.

"Because I ran and didn't tell him," she answers quietly, and all I can think of is how much I want to beat the shit out of him. She isn't the type to run for no reason, she ran because she was scared. I can see that in her eyes.

I've fought lots of men in The Cage, and I see that fear in their eyes every time. Sometimes it's right at the start because they are smart and know they won't win. For others, there's no fear at the start, just arrogance, and then, when I've beaten them and I'm about to knock them out, the fear is there.

"What happened?" I ask her gently, knowing she doesn't have to tell me.

"The night I tried to leave him to come here, he caught me. He went mad, throwing stuff around the room and then told me I wasn't leaving. I got brave and told him to screw himself before trying to run out the door," she says quietly.

"You're safe with me," I whisper when she stops talking.

"He caught me on the stairs and threw me to the floor. Next thing I knew, he kicked me and I fell down the stairs, hitting my head when I stopped at the bottom. He tried to . . . well, he tried to force himself on me. While he was ripping my jeans off, I picked up the glass football statue my brother, Ace, had left by the bottom of the stairs and slammed it over his head. I don't know if I killed him because I just got up, grabbed my suitcase, and ran," she says, angrily wiping her eyes as I rest my hand on her shoulder. I can't say I'm surprised, but this is worse than what I was expecting.

"Tilly," I whisper, and she looks up at me, only for a second before looking away.

"Let's be clear on something, okay?" I ask her. I slide my hand over her cheek and move a little closer on the bed, so our faces are inches away as I talk to her. I rub my thumb over her cheek gently.

"I hope you killed that fucker. I hope he is dead, and if he comes anywhere near you or your baby, I will make sure he never looks at you again," I promise her.

"Why do you protect me?" she asks.

"I feel like you're mine to protect," I whisper, freezing as she kisses me.

Her lips brush against mine, reminding me how she tastes like sweets and how soft her lips are. I don't hold back this time as I kiss her back, and she melts into me. I roll myself over her, holding my weight with my hands as we kiss.

"Harley." She moans as I push my body into her gently and slowly kiss down her neck.

I stop and look up at her, watching as she smiles lightly. That smile does me in, it makes me like her more, and my breath stops. If I take this any farther, if I let myself be with her and then something happens to me in that fight, she would be alone and I would hurt her. She doesn't deserve that.

"Why did you stop?" she asks.

"I can't take this farther, not yet. Remember, no promises." I tell her, making her frown because she can't understand.

"No promises . . . but can't we just–" She sighs, pushing her body into mine, and it takes a hell of a lot of willpower to resist her. I shake my head, gently kissing her again.

"Is it because I'm pregnant? Does that freak you out?" she asks, and I laugh.

"Not at all. This isn't because I don't want you, because I do," I say, knowing she can feel how turned on I am.

"I promised myself no serious relationships until The Cage is behind me. I can't be with you and risk my life there. I want to be honest with you. I'm no good for a girl like you," I tell her, watching as her face goes from sad to angry.

"That's a load of bullshit. You can't choose whether I like you or not. You can't time falling for someone," she says.

"It's not. You need a family man, someone better

than me. I won't drag you down to my level, Tilly, but I will protect you," I tell her firmly.

"So you will keep me safe but won't be with me?" she asks, and I nod.

I slide off the bed, only looking back once at Tilly, wishing things were fucking different. The big fight is coming up soon, and I doubt I'm going to survive it anyway. I'm going to make sure she is protected, that my whole family is. I won't let her fall for me only to have her heart broken.

"This is a mistake, Harley," she says gently, before rolling over in bed and facing away from me.

It is a mistake, a mistake because I've already fallen for her.

# CHAPTER 14
HARLEY

## TWO MONTHS LATER...

"Congratulations, Tilly. She is so beautiful," Izzy says as she looks down at my little girl in my arms. The midwives just finished cleaning me up after I gave birth, and I can't look away from her. She looks like my mum, with her red hair and bright-blue eyes. She doesn't look like him, for which I'm thankful. I finally get what the books say about that instant love you feel when you look at your child, that bond. It feels like my heart is going to burst with love as I stare down at her, knowing I would do anything to keep her safe. I don't regret a single moment of my life, not anymore, because I would have never have gotten here. I lean down and kiss her forehead, loving the new baby smell she has. I swear nothing smells as lovely as she does in this moment.

"Thank you, she is," I reply, watching as she yawns. Every movement she makes is cute. There is no other way to describe her.

"You need to call your parents, they should know, and your brothers, too. They love you, Tilly," Izzy says gently, and I look over at her. I know she means well, but the idea of having anyone from France near my child right now is making me paranoid.

"The moment I tell them, he will find me. I've spoken to them twice in the last two months, and they know we ended badly. They promised not to tell anyone where I am, but I know he is still friends with Devon," I say, thinking of my brother and how I wish I could talk to him. I glance at the fox tattoo on my wrist, knowing things are not going to get better overnight like I want them to.

"He won't ever go near you; he would have to go through me first," Harley says, coming into the room, looking tired but relieved all at the same time.

After our kisses all those months ago, we have become closer friends, and he has never been anything else to me. He takes me out on dates and meals all the time. He buys me baby things and makes me food when I am too tired to cook. But we never talk about us. I almost hate that he seems to have forgotten those kisses when it's all I can think about.

Harley is dressed far more casually than I'm used to seeing him, with just jeans and a grey jumper on. His hair is bundled at the back of his head, and he gives me a happy look.

"You can't promise that, Harley," I respond as he comes in and sits in the chair by the bed. He looks over at my daughter and then up to me.

"I can," he tells me gently.

Harley waited outside throughout the whole labour, and Izzy was holding my hand throughout it in here. The labour was short, *thank God*, but painful. Harley wanted to come in, but I think I just needed it to be Izzy and me. I was already sad my mother couldn't be here, and Izzy is the only thing close to family I have here. I was surprised Harley didn't mind, he told me to do whatever made me happy and that he would be nearby. Then he kissed my forehead as a long contraction came on, and the midwives took me into the birthing unit.

"Have you thought of a name?" Izzy asks, and I shake my head.

"I couldn't decide on one, so not yet," I respond, and then someone knocks at the door. Izzy gets up and goes to open it slightly before I can hear Allie.

"Can I come in?" she asks.

"Yes," I reply back.

I've gotten closer to Allie in the last few months and consider her a good friend. I can see why Izzy and Maisy love her so much.

"Maisy wanted to come, but she isn't getting much sleep with the baby kicking her, so I told her to rest," Allie tells me.

Maisy only has a month left until they meet their own baby girl. I still remember Sebastian's shocked face when he came back from the scan with Maisy. Saying Sebastian was shocked might have been an understatement, and I kind of wanted that same feeling for myself, which is why I never found out the sex of my baby during my scans.

"That's okay," I say, watching as Allie walks over and looks down at my baby.

"She's a real beauty, with that red hair and button nose," she says gently, and I nod, looking at her.

"Thank you, she is."

"Why don't we go get some drinks and food? I need to call Blake to let him know we can't go on that secret trip he planned," Izzy says.

"Another secret trip?" I ask, knowing he has taken her on three now.

"Yes, something always seems to go wrong on each trip. The first time we went on a boat and it was lovely with lights and everything. Then the boat engine caught caught fire and we had to get off the boat.

"The second date was the beach. Again lovely, but halfway through the date, it started to pour down with rain, and then lightning hit a nearby tree, setting it on fire.

"And the third secret date, we didn't even get to because the car broke down on the way there."

"So unlucky," I say, watching as Harley is grinning at the floor and trying not to laugh.

"I don't get why he keeps planning all these things, I'm happy with a normal meal." Izzy laughs. "But it is sweet."

Allie kisses my cheek before leaving with Izzy, and Harley stands up.

"Can I hold her?" he asks, and I lift my arms a little so Harley can pick her up off me. Seeing him holding my little girl is beyond cute, even more so when he starts rocking her gently.

"She looks like you," he says.

"That's a good thing," I respond, and his green eyes stare down at me.

"I'm proud of you, doing all this alone. You're so strong," he tells me.

"I'm not alone, you're here. I know I will be in the future, but for now, I really appreciate all your help," I say, and Harley goes to respond when the baby wakes up with a small cry. Harley hands her back to me after placing a kiss on her forehead.

"I'm not going anywhere, not now or ever. Not unless you ask me to, Tilly," he says, but I know he can't promise me that. He hasn't won the fight yet, and he won't even tell me when it is. All Harley has done is train and work out, getting ready for this fight. His arms are so muscular, bigger than before, and every part of him looks prepared for a fight now.

"Do you need anything?" he asks, and I shake my head, pulling my eyes away from him.

"No. I have a bottle ready and everything in that bag you brought in." I nod my head toward the bag sitting on a chair in the room.

I know breastfeeding is better for the baby, but I want to bottle feed. I know it's my choice in the end, and it's something I feel more comfortable with. I spoke a lot to the midwives about it, and they said that some women choose the same as I have.

"Will you let me feed her? Only if you want," he says, almost stumbling a little on his words as he looks nervous. I nod, watching as he opens one of the pre-made bottles and puts a feeding top on it. Harley comes and takes my daughter from me and starts feeding her in his arms as he sits on the edge of the bed.

"Why are you here? With me? I don't know many

men who would want to help their roommate with their first baby, and you've made it clear that's all I can be to you," I say, ignoring the sharp shot of pain I feel at even saying those words. I know my hormones are likely making me a little emotional at the moment, but I'm trying to be normal.

"I'm not going anywhere, I'm here for you. I know she isn't mine, but I want you to know that I'm here," he tells me gently.

"Is it because of our kisses? I don't want you to think you owe me anything. I get that you don't want to be with me, but please don't help me out of guilt. I plan to move out as soon as I can–"

"Stop," he tells me, shifting on the bed so he can look at me, his eyes daring me to look away. "All I've wanted since our last kiss is to kiss you again. Every damn time I look at you. I haven't stopped thinking about it, about you. I don't want you to move out, but there is a month until my last fight."

"When is the fight exactly? The date?" I ask, wondering if I can get him to tell me now, but at least I know it's in a month, which isn't long at all. Izzy said it was weird none of them had been fighting in the last few months. She said none of them would talk about it, and that's suspicious enough. This fight must be something else.

"One last fight, and my family will be free. I just

need to win it," Harley says, but it is so quiet I'm sure he's just talking to himself and not to me.

"Is that why you're always working out?" I ask him.

"Maybe I just like to work out," he suggests, but he doesn't look at me as he says it.

"Who is this fight against?" I ask him.

"It doesn't matter," he says.

"Why doesn't it? You told me you have never lost a fight, so you won't lose this one," I say, hope filling me that he may finally be free of his past. That he may eventually have a future.

"I might," he says, the words causing me to go silent as I look at him, staring down at my daughter in his arms.

"No," I reply quietly, and Harley doesn't say a word.

# CHAPTER 15

## HARLEY

"Why don't you go and take her into the lounge, and I will get the bags?" I tell Tilly, who looks up at me with tired eyes.

I'm glad she is finally out of the hospital and is home again. The new baby has been struggling to sleep with the noise of the hospital ward, and I've been by her side, trying to help. She still hasn't chosen a name for the beautiful baby she is holding, but we have all taken to calling her 'baby girl' for now. I know it's difficult with a new baby, just from helping Maisy and Sebastian with Jake.

"Okay." She nods, walking off, and I open the door to go and get her maternity bags out of the car.

I stop in my tracks when I see a man and an older woman standing at the door. The man is a little younger than me, with dark-brown hair and a serious expression. The woman has long, red hair up in a ponytail, and she must be in her late forties as her roots are going grey. When she looks up at me, I know who she is straight away from her eyes.

"You're Tilly's mum?" I ask, and she nods, putting her hands on her hips.

"Where is my bloody runaway daughter?" she asks.

"Tilly!" the man shouts, looking like he wants to try to push me out of the way, but that's not happening until I know who he is. If this is Tilly's ex, I'm going to kill him for turning up here, and I'm sure he can tell my thoughts from the strange expression he gives me.

"Devon?" I hear Tilly ask from behind me.

I move slightly so Devon can walk into the house, and he hugs Tilly. I look behind her to see the lounge door open, and I know Tilly must have put the baby in the Moses basket for a nap.

"Don't you dare run off on us like that again. It took me ages to find you, sis," he says, and she moves away. I watch as Tilly and her mum stare at each other for a long time before Tilly walks over and hugs her mum.

"I don't believe a word you said over the phone,

not a word, Matilda," she scolds her daughter, and I finally learn her real name.

"Don't call me that. Jesus, it's Tilly," Tilly says, rolling her eyes and making her brother laugh.

"We need to talk, and you have some explaining to do," her mother says, and Tilly sighs. I walk over, placing my arm on her shoulder. She doesn't stop me.

"I'm Harley King." I offer a hand to Tilly's mum, who shakes it firmly.

"Linda Fox."

"I'm Devon Fox. Are you dating my sister?" Devon asks, walking over.

Something about his name sounds familiar. I remember Izzy telling me she dated one of Tilly's brothers before we met her.

"Yes, and I believe you dated my sister, Izzy? I remember her saying your name," I reply as we shake hands.

"You're one of the new brothers," Devon comments, but I doubt he wants an answer as a baby's cry fills the room.

Tilly moves away from me and walks into the lounge. We all follow, watching her walk over to the baby, who is in the Moses basket.

"Whose baby is that?" Devon asks, stopping by the door in shock, and their mum is just standing, staring at Tilly, who rocks her baby gently. I'm pretty sure the red hair and the way Tilly holds her baby are all the answer he needs, but they both seem to stay quiet, waiting for Tilly to actually say the words.

"My baby," Tilly says quietly, and Linda makes a small, sobbing sound.

She walks over and stands next to Tilly, looking down at the baby. I watch as she lifts a shaky hand and touches the side of the baby's face gently. Linda reaches into her pocket, pulling out a tissue and wiping her face.

"Is the baby Daniel's? I mean, he should know!" Devon says, and a look of panic fills Tilly's face as she glances at me. I can actually see her thinking about running away already, and I can't let her do that. I won't let her leave.

"The baby girl is mine," I say and walk over to Tilly, wrapping an arm around her waist as she tries to hide the shock she is clearly feeling.

"Why didn't you tell me?"

"I don't know. I'm sorry I didn't, but I would appreciate it if you don't tell my ex about where I am. It would only upset him, Devon," she says, and Devon nods, looking between us.

I don't know if he believes what we are telling him, but something seems to change as he looks at me. I stand firm as we stare at each other, wondering if he is going to attempt to punch me, or do something else stupid.

"Fine. He is still not over you, but as long as you're happy," Devon eventually says, and some part of me is furious that he is sticking up for that asshole. But I know he doesn't know what Daniel is really like; what he tried to do to his sister.

"I am."

"Well, I want to hold my niece then, what's her name?" Devon asks, but Linda doesn't say a word as she stares at me for a long time. Her stare seems to be figuring something out, and I doubt she is as quick to believe our story as Devon is. I'm just wondering if she is going to say something now, or later.

"Can I have a moment alone with my daughter?" Linda asks, and Tilly nods. Devon takes the baby from Tilly, and I lead him out of the room, shutting the door behind us.

"Fair warning, I promise to shove your head up your arse if you hurt her," Devon says, his voice low as he speaks so he doesn't upset the baby, but the protectiveness makes me like him already.

"Funny, I said the same thing to the guy dating Izzy now," I say, and he chuckles.

"She happy?" he asks me just as the door opens.

Izzy and Blake walk in, and Izzy stops in her tracks when she sees Devon.

"I wondered when you lot would turn up," Izzy says, and Devon laughs.

Blake doesn't look happy as Devon walks over and slides an arm around Izzy's waist, giving her a side hug.

"Blake, this is Devon, one of Tilly's brothers," Izzy introduces them, and Blake just nods.

"Nice to meet you. Izzy, you could have called to let us know about, well . . ." He looks down at the sleeping baby in his arms.

"It wasn't my secret to tell, Dev," she replies.

"It's still a big one. Dad is going to go mad when he finds out. So will Ace and Grayson," he comments, and I guess they must be Tilly's other brothers.

"How is Grayson? I heard he got married and had a kid," Izzy asks.

"Yep and divorced. He has full custody of my nephew now and is moving here soon," he says. It looks like the Foxes are moving into town. I hope they realise how much of a fucked-up town this place is. They may regret moving here after all.

"And Ace? Is he, what . . . fifteen now?" she asks.

"Yeah, and an asshole," Devon replies, making Izzy laugh.

"He was always like that, even as a kid," Izzy replies.

The baby starts crying lightly, and I hold my hands out, watching as Devon slides her into my arms. I head to the kitchen to sort out a bottle, while the others follow.

"Isn't it weird that we now share a niece?" Devon comments.

"My daughter is lovely, isn't she?" I say to Blake and Izzy, who give me wide-eyed, confused looks. Thank god they quickly realise and blank their expressions.

"Yes, lovely," Izzy says, and Blake shakes his head with a small smirk.

"I would stay, but the moving vans are coming today and I can't leave Ace to sort the stuff out by himself. I doubt he will even answer the damn door," Devon comments.

"It's nice to see you again, Devon," Izzy replies, and he nods, looking between Blake and Izzy for a second, but I see it.

"I'm glad you're happy," he says, before walking to the door.

"She is," Blake says, his words possessive, and Devon gives him one nod. Some kind of understanding between them.

"Tell Tilly I will be over tomorrow," he tells me.

I have a feeling her family is going to be around a lot now.

# CHAPTER 16
## TILLY

"Are you disappointed in me?" I ask quietly as my mum sits down on the sofa, and I go to sit next to her.

I'm still in shock that she turned up here, and that Harley just claimed to be the father of my baby. The man who says he can't be with me is being there for me in every damn way anyway. I doubt he sees it like that, though.

"No . . . just a little shocked, Tilly," she says, leaning back into the sofa and looking around the room.

"This is a nice house, does your boyfriend own it?" she asks me.

"Yes, and his brother, Luke, lives here, too. Izzy stays over sometimes."

"I can't wait to see little Elizabeth. I've really

missed her, it must be nice to have a friend around," she says, and I nod.

There's an awkward silence that spreads between us, and I don't know how to break it. I can't exactly say sorry for not telling her and yet, I don't know what to say to her. I don't like seeing my mum like this, so worried and confused.

"Is Dad okay?" I ask, actually wondering why he isn't here. My dad is not the type to let his wife fight his battles, and I know from the three phone calls I've answered that he isn't happy with me.

"He had business to clear up before the move, so he won't be here until tomorrow," she replies.

"Oh."

"Ace misses his sister, so does Grayson," she tells me, and I nod, knowing I miss them too. I've always been close to my brothers. We aren't far from each other in age.

"Why didn't you tell me? Why did you run?" she asks me the second question before I can reply to the first.

"I–" I start to say, and she cuts me off.

"Devon may be an idiot and know nothing about pregnancy, but I've had four children. You're pregnant for nine months, and you didn't leave our house until about four months ago, so there is no way that little baby is Harley's unless you cheated on Daniel in France. Now . . . you want to say the baby is early to your brothers, or even your dad, to carry on with this lie, then fine, but not with me," she says firmly.

"The baby is Daniel's," I say, hating to even mention his name out loud or admitting that even a part of my sweet, baby girl belongs to him. I will spend the rest of my life making sure she is nothing like him at all.

"Why doesn't he know?" she asks me.

I look at my mum, with her red hair like mine and the smart look in her eyes as she thinks everything over. I know I should tell her, but the words don't seem to want to leave my lips. I end up thinking back to Harley, how he told me everything about him, and he wasn't frightened to do that. I need to be strong like him. At the end of the day, I didn't do anything wrong.

"The night I left, he hurt me, Mum, and he tried to–" I take a deep breath. "He tried to rape me. I ran away because I don't want him anywhere near my baby or me. Harley is just protecting me," I say.

"Oh, Tilly," she says, pulling me into a hug.

We both stay still for a long time as she cries on my shoulder, and I don't know what else to say. Part of me feels like crying, and another huge part of me just wants to forget France. I can't even speak the damn language anyway, not like my brothers can.

"Where is Daniel? He isn't coming here, is he?" I ask, knowing that if she says he is, I will have to leave. I don't want to, I don't want to leave Harley. That arrogant man makes me like him more and more every day.

"No, he stayed. He wanted to come, but he couldn't leave his work. Honestly, he moved out not long after you and only saw Devon weekly," she tells me, and part of me is relieved that he wasn't in their life.

"He is evil, Mum; he hurt me once before and used to control me. Everything from what I wore, to where I could go, and when I was away from him, he was obsessively calling my phone and accusing me of cheating on him when I got home," I tell her, and her eyes widen.

"He won't come here because if he does, I'm going to kill him, and your dad is going to help," she tells me. I don't doubt her; my mum can be scary as hell at times.

"Dad doesn't need to go back to prison, and I don't want to lose my mum, either, but Harley won't let him near me. You've seen the man, he is built like a machine, and Daniel would have to be mad to try to go near me now," I reassure her.

"He is a handsome man and a good man to be at

your side like this. He's a keeper," my mum says, waggling her eyebrows.

"And a complicated man," I respond, making her smile.

"The best ones always are, but he is there for you. Most men would run," she says, and I know she's right.

"Harley wouldn't run, he isn't like that. His very nature is to be protective. He brought all of his brothers up since their dad died," I tell her.

"That poor boy," my mum says.

"And then, he took Izzy and me in, knowing about the baby, too," I say.

Mum nods, looking around the room and to the Moses basket. Harley bought the Moses basket and set it all in here for me. He put my favourite bed blanket on the sofa, and there is even a drink left out for me on the side. He must have done all this, getting ready for me to come home.

"Does he know about Daniel?" she asks me quietly.

"Yes, he was the first person I could actually tell. He makes me feel safe, and he understands me. Well, we understand each other . . . I can't explain it," I say.

"I don't have to understand it, only you two do. You know I'm a big believer in fate, and sometimes fate leads you to the only person who can understand you, sweetheart," she says, placing her hand over mine.

"Mrs. Fox, I mean Linda," Izzy says as she opens the door and runs into the room. My mum stands up to hug her as she and Blake come in, shutting the door behind them.

"Oh, Elizabeth, it's so lovely to see you. You have grown so much since I last saw you," my mum says as Izzy pulls away.

"I missed you, too," she says with a big smile.

"You look the image of your mother, she would be so proud of you. At university and settling down," she tells Izzy, who gives her a small, sad smile. I know she misses her mum every day, but my mum is right, they do look alike.

"Now . . . who is this handsome man?" Mum asks Izzy, who laughs as Blake comes over.

"My boyfriend, Blake . . . Blake, this is Linda, Tilly's mum."

"A pleasure to meet you," Blake says as he shakes Mum's hand.

"The pleasure is all mine," Mum says, winking at Izzy, who laughs. Blake looks a little worried as we all start laughing.

My family is here.

## CHAPTER 17
TILLY

"You have a baby, that baby?" My dad repeats for the third time since I explained everything, pointing at my daughter in her pushchair by the door.

Harley is standing next to her and gives me a sympathetic look. I haven't even had a chance to introduce him yet. I know my mum told him and has been trying to calm him down all morning before we got here. I guess it's not every day you find out your only daughter has a baby that you didn't know about.

"Yes," I repeat.

"Why didn't you tell us?" he asks me, standing with his hands on his hips and glaring down at me.

My dad is a scary person, and he is as big as Harley, with his muscular arms and serious expression. All the kids at school used to be scared of him, except for Izzy, who knew he is just a big teddy bear . . . usually. Except at times like this.

"Darling, Tilly isn't a child anymore, and yes, she should have told us, but does it matter? We have a granddaughter," my mum says, her tone soothing. It always seems to be able to calm my dad down.

"I know she isn't a child," he says with a sigh, coming over to me. My dad picks me up into a large hug and then lets go.

"Right . . . if you get pregnant again, I want to know. Now, who the hell is the giant by the door?" he asks, pointing at Harley.

Harley walks over and offers his hand to shake. "Harley King."

"Jerald Fox," my dad says, shaking his hand.

When Harley lets go and takes my hand in his, I'm a little surprised by his touch, but I don't comment on it.

"You the dad?" he asks.

"Yes. I met Tilly in France when Izzy told me her friend lived near," he says, repeating the lie we came up with to tell my family. I can't tell them the whole truth, and this is just easier.

"You cheated on poor Daniel?" my dad asks with a disappointed look.

"That's private, Mr. Fox," Harley says, and my dad turns his glare on him.

"Why don't we say hello to our grandchild? You can go and have a look around," Mum says, breaking the tension a little, but Dad doesn't look happy. His gaze seems to soften when he sees my mum pick up my baby girl from her pram, and he rubs his face with his hands.

"Go on, then, I have a baby to meet," he says, and I quickly walk away with Harley.

"Okay, I've been in a lot of fights and met people that are huge and fucking scary, but your dad is . . ." Harley whispers, making me laugh.

"Yeah, I know, imagine getting told off by him as a kid." I laugh, and Harley gives me a gentle smile.

"I would have preferred that over my father."

"I guess I understand that," I respond as we walk around the bottom half of the house, seeing no one.

The house is huge, with two lounges and a big kitchen. A much bigger house than we ever had before, and I briefly wonder where they got the money for a house like this before Harley speaks.

"My dad liked to beat the shit out of my brothers and me, training us to fight in The Cage for him. I don't know if Izzy told you all that, but yeah, he got us into fighting to start with," he says quietly, and I tug on his hand to stop him from walking up the stairs we find in the middle of the corridor we entered.

"I'm sorry, I never realised he trained you. I should have guessed," I say, and he smiles at me.

"I never felt sorry for myself, but I did for my brothers. I tried to protect them, and I would have done anything to do that," he says. "Tilly, I wish you would listen to me."

"Listen to what?" I ask gently.

"When I say I'm no good for you, I mean it. I fucked and fought to protect my brothers, I'm not a good man. I don't get why you keep fighting for me, for us, Tilly," he says, moving closer to me. I take a step back, my back hitting the wall, and he moves to stand in front of me.

"What if I don't want a good man? What if I want you?" I ask.

He lowers his face close to mine before he whispers, "That would be a bad idea, siren."

"It wouldn't," I reply, leaning up and brushing my lips against his, not caring about what he says. Harley King may think he isn't good for me, but I know he is worth fighting for. He resists me for only a second before he takes control of the kiss and is pushing his hard body into mine.

"Fuck . . . not what I expected to see this early in

the morning," my youngest brother's voice comes from near us, and we break away from the kiss.

I turn to see Ace standing at the bottom of the stairs, his black hair is everywhere, and his blue eyes look tired. He has a cigarette hanging out of his mouth, a leather jacket on, and faded blue jeans.

"Are you smoking?"

"Says you, who got pregnant and ran away. Sis . . . I think you're winning the title for the most irresponsible one out of us, no?" he asks, and I glare at him.

"You're such a rude, little shit, Ace," I comment, and he laughs.

"Missed you, too, Tills," he says and walks past us both, looking at Harley for a second.

"You fight in that cage? I saw the odds for the one coming up. Don't die, yeah?" he says and then turns, walking out of the corridor.

"How did your brother see the odds?" Harley asks me, and I have no idea.

"What are the odds?" I ask Harley.

"You don't want to know, siren," he tells me and then walks away from me before I can ask him anything else.

## CHAPTER 18

HARLEY

"What happened?" I ask Blake when he shuts the kitchen door behind him with a tired sigh and not the happy grin I expected to see.

Sebastian and Elliot look over as they stop what they were doing. I stop cooking the pasta I was making for us all to celebrate Izzy and Blake's engagement, knowing they'd be home soon from their weekend away. The poor dude has taken her on five dates now to propose, and every one of them has gone wrong. I seriously didn't think this one could go wrong, but the look on his face says something did.

"I went to ask when I realised how much of an idiot I am. I left the damn ring box in the car. The car the valet drove away," he says, and I mentally sigh.

"That's unlucky, man," Sebastian says, trying not to laugh, and I whack him on the arm.

"Just plan something else, or just ask randomly. I mean, you could tell her all the fucking romantic things you tried to plan," Elliot says.

"Coming from the guy who would ask Allie to marry him on his bike," Blake responds drily, looking stressed.

"What's wrong with that idea?" Elliot asks, and none of us answer. There is so much wrong with that idea, and I doubt Allie would be happy.

"Let's dish up and have a nice meal anyway, but I am sorry, Blake; you just seem to have the worst luck," I comment.

"I got lucky when I met Izzy, so I knew the universe had to mess with me somehow," Blake says with a laugh.

"How long until the fight?" Blake asks me, causing the kitchen to suddenly go silent.

"Two weeks."

"Fuck, I didn't know it was that soon," Blake says, and my brothers look away.

They have given up trying to convince me not to do this. That we should all run from here and leave this village in our past. I know they would get up and leave everything, with their girlfriends and children following, but I couldn't expect them to do that.

They know there really isn't any way of us getting out of it because we would be looking over our shoulders for the rest of our lives. This is a chance to actually escape.

We all finish sorting the food out, hearing the girls laughing in the living room. It's nice knowing Tilly is really settling in with our family. I don't know when it became hers as much as mine, but I know I wouldn't be able to let her out of my life.

"Is it strange having a baby in the house that isn't yours?" Elliot asks me as we carry food into the dining room.

"No. I don't see her like that, but I wish Tilly would name her. Calling her 'baby girl' for the last two weeks hasn't been easy."

"I bet," Elliot replies, but he doesn't look at me. "Dude . . . maybe you should ask her to move into her parents. I don't get why she is staying here now that they have moved here. They have a massive house, and she should be with family," Elliot adds, but I don't look at him as Tilly stops in the doorway, hearing every word. Her hurt-filled eyes meet mine, and she turns around, walking out.

"Tilly, wait!" I shout at her back as she walks away, and I glare at Elliot who holds his hands up before I follow her through the house.

She stops inside the conservatory, which no one

goes into, and watches the rain pouring down outside. I close the door behind me, looking her over. Tilly is wearing jeans and a white top, which makes her look like she didn't just have a baby. Her long, red hair is loose and wavy, begging me to touch it.

"Do you want me to move out?" she asks quietly, but her voice echoes around the conservatory.

"No," I reply with one word, but it means everything as I watch as she turns to look at me.

I don't move as she walks over, placing both her hands on my chest and looking up at me. Tilly raises her hand and pushes a bit of my hair behind my ear before grazing her finger across my cheek. Only the sound of our heavy breathing fills the room.

"When are you going to stop pushing me away?" she asks.

"I'm not good for you, Tilly, but I can't let you go," I reply, leaning down to kiss her. I can't resist her anymore.

Tilly moans as she relaxes into the kiss, and her hands go into my hair. I pull her up to me, kissing her harder and loving the way she moves her body against mine.

"I can't, not yet," she says, breaking away, and I know she means because it's not long after her labour, not that she doesn't want to be with me.

"I'm sorry, I'm fucking sorry I've been avoiding

this, us. Not anymore, Tilly," I say, watching as her blue eyes watch me. "You're mine now, and I'm not pushing you away anymore. You're the reason I'm going to win that fight in two weeks."

"You're still fighting? It's in two weeks?" she asks, her voice nervous, and I hate that I have to fight. That I can't just walk away from it all. I can't do that to my brothers.

"I don't have a choice, Tilly," I reply. There's a knock on the door behind me, and I open it to Maisy, who smiles.

"Sorry, but the food is ready and everyone is waiting," she says.

Maisy has a huge bump now, and there is a planned birth for two weeks' time. It's the day after the fight, and I can't wait to be able to see their baby when I win.

"Where's Jake?" I ask her, knowing I forgot to ask earlier.

"With my dad. He popped over and Jake was napping. I didn't want to wake him up as he was up all night with a new tooth coming through," Maisy responds as I shut the door behind Tilly.

"Are you excited for the baby to come?" I ask her about the planned birth as we walk down the corridor, and I don't let go of Tilly's hand. I'm not hiding how I feel about her anymore.

"Very," she says, rubbing a hand over her bump.

We walk into the dining room to see everyone is seated, and Izzy hands the baby monitor to Tilly before sitting down. I lean over and kiss Tilly gently on the lips before I sit next to her, and I'm aware of how silent the room has gone as I look at her blushed cheeks.

"About time," Sebastian mutters, and I look over to see them all staring at us.

"When did this happen, and how did I not realise?" Izzy asks.

"Just now, and I don't know," Tilly answers with a smile.

"Damn . . . I owe you fifty now," Elliot says to Luke, who laughs.

"Me, too," Sebastian nods.

"Why wasn't I included in this bet?" Izzy asks, making us all laugh.

Allie comes into the room with two drinks and takes the seat next to Elliot. "So . . . what did I miss?" she asks.

"Those two are together," Elliot waves a hand at us as he speaks.

"Dammit. Fifty quid went," Allie mutters, and I can't help but laugh at her.

"Best bet I ever made," Luke says, but he goes silent as Emilia walks into the room.

Emilia is one of Izzy, Blake, and Allie's roommates, and there's something weird going on between her and Luke. Everyone has mentioned it, but if you ask them, they won't talk about each other. Emilia sits next to Tilly.

"You dyed your hair black, it looks really nice," Tilly comments, and Emilia smiles.

"Wanted a change," she shrugs.

"Like the new tattoos, too?" Allie responds as I get some pasta for my plate. We all start helping ourselves to the food as Emilia talks.

"Only one or two," she comments, her cheeks going a little red.

"Why didn't you come to me? I would have done them for you," Luke says.

"I didn't want to, but thanks," she responds, her tone curt and short with him.

"Why not?" he asks, his tone is downright pissed off, and I raise my eyebrows at Tilly as she gives me a wide-eyed look.

"Because, despite what you think, Luke, the world doesn't revolve around you," Emilia snaps.

"Guys," Izzy tries to break up the argument, but it doesn't work.

"I never said it did, I only offered to help you," he comments.

"I don't need your damn help," Emilia says, standing up and walking out of the room. Luke pushes his chair out and follows her out.

"Who wants to make a bet that they will be with each other soon?" Elliot asks, breaking the tension.

"I'm in," Tilly responds, and I laugh.

"Yeah, me, too," I agree. There's something there between them.

"Nah, I don't think so," Sebastian says, shaking his head.

"Why?" I ask.

"They argue too much, and they are both so young," Sebastian says, and he has a point. Out of all of us, Luke is the youngest, but then, I saw the way he looked at Emilia.

"So? We met younger than them," Maisy answers.

"True, but I don't know," Sebastian shakes his head.

"I totally think they have already done it," Allie says.

"Why?" Izzy responds.

"Just something she said once." Allie shrugs, and then the baby monitor starts beeping before the sound of the baby crying comes through. Tilly goes to get up, and I stop her by placing my hand on her shoulder.

"I'll go," I say, knowing Tilly has been up half the night with the baby. I tried to help, but she only seemed to want her mum.

"Thank you," Tilly says, and I get up, walking out of the room.

I go straight upstairs and into Tilly's room. The bad smell hits me straight away, and I know what the problem is. Once I change the baby's nappy, I sit in the nursing chair and rock her in my arms. I look down at her cute, little nose and her little strands of red hair. She looks every bit like her mother. I rock the baby until she falls asleep on my chest and lean my head back on the chair. She might not be my daughter, but it's starting to feel like I would do anything to protect both her and her mum.

# CHAPTER 19
## TILLY

"Is this your way of distracting me from tonight?" I ask Izzy, who nervously laughs as she pushes her long, blond hair over her shoulder, looking away from me.

"No, of course not," she says, proving my point that it is.

"I know Harley is fighting tonight, and I know you think distracting me by taking me out shopping for baby clothes is going to stop me from worrying or something, but it's not going to work. I can't stop thinking about tonight, and every part of me just wants to tie my giant to a chair," I tell her, and she gives me a worried look as we walk through the shop.

"Don't you think I worry?" Izzy comments.

"I know you do, it's just . . . I can't lose him," I say

when we get outside the shop, and Izzy puts an arm around me.

"I feel the same way every time one of them fights, but these are the Kings. Since I met them, I've known they are strong, and they walk out of that cage every . . . damn . . . time. This is the last one, Tilly, and then, they are all free from their past, and Harley finally has someone waiting for him," she tells me, and her eyes, so much like Harley's, watch me with concern.

Izzy looks as tired as I do, her eyes dark and her clothes half ironed, same as me. I woke up to find Harley in the gym, beating the crap out of a punching bag. He didn't even notice me there, not as I looked at the scars on his back, which looked like knife cuts, noticing the way his muscles almost hides the scars. I never interrupted him because I didn't know what to say. Watching him fight a punching bag like that made me realise how he has to fight tonight.

"I just didn't expect to finally be happy with an amazing guy and then have to watch him do something that could kill him," I say.

"I know, Tilly. I wish I could tell you not to worry and that you're going to get your happy ending, but I can't. I'm just as scared as you," she says.

A woman walks past with her baby in a

pushchair, and I smile. My mum and dad have my baby for the day, and I've still not been able to come up with a name for her. I actually have to before the six-week deadline to register her birth, and yet, here I am, not choosing her name and calling her 'baby girl.' My parents have actually said 'baby girl' suits her, so I know I need to change it before my poor daughter gets stuck with that nickname for the rest of her life. That would not be a good nickname when she is a teenager.

Baby girl has the whole family in love with her; well, make that two families. She has the Foxes and Kings wrapped around her tiny fingers. Even my brothers take turns holding her, and I actually saw Ace kissing her forehead yesterday when I took her over to see them.

"I just think you could use some girl time and, also, I want to hear about how you and my brother... Well, actually, no I don't," she says, shuddering a little.

"You want to know how we got together?" I ask, laughing a little but getting what she is asking me.

"Yes, exactly," she says, thankful for my save.

"I think it's just because I get him. There isn't anything else to it. And, for your information, we haven't done anything but kiss," I say, though, not for my lack of trying. I know Harley doesn't want to take things farther than kissing, but it's teasing to have all these kisses and nothing else.

"Really?" Izzy asks, with a little bit of shock.

"He doesn't want to be with me and then hurt me if he doesn't return from The Cage. He still kisses me, but we don't share a bed. It's so frustrating as he is so–"

"Brother, remember?" she says with a scrunched-up face. "No, I kind of get why he hasn't taken things farther with you. To him, you mean more than just sex," she says. "But no more talk about Harley like that. I see him as a dad figure."

We walk around a few more of the shops, and I buy some new baby clothes and some boots.

"Should we get some lunch?" Izzy asks, nodding her head toward the café on the other side of the shopping centre. There are plants lined down the middle and it says the local school children have been planting them. For everything this village has hidden, like The Cage and the way Harley told me the police act around here, there are good things. I guess the motto that the good comes with the bad applies to this place.

"Izzy, do you know how to get to The Cage?" I ask her randomly, and she gives me a shocked look.

"Yes, but I can't take you there. Not after what I told you. Arthur is dangerous," she tells me.

"I know, just some part of me wants to be there for him. He said he wouldn't take me there, but if you told me the way . . ."

"I agree with Harley here. The Cage is dangerous, Tilly," she tells me, and I sigh. I knew her answer before she even said it.

I look back over at the café, seeing a wave of blond hair on a tall guy. He is standing with sunglasses on, his arms crossed as he watches me from the other side of the line of plants in the middle of the shopping centre. I know it's him, as he looks my way, and fear fills every part of me. I zone out, not listening to Izzy talk as I stop walking just to stare at Daniel through the plants. At least, I think it's him. Even thinking his name scares me. A couple of people pass in front of the plants, and then he is gone, making me snap out of it and I step backward.

"Tilly?" Izzy shakes my arm. "You're shaking, what did you see?" Izzy asks, looking around, and I shake my head.

"Daniel was here, I'm sure of it," I mutter, and Izzy wraps an arm around me.

"I doubt he was, you must have just been seeing things," she says, and I shake my head. Knowing she might be right, but I can't shake the feeling that it was him here.

"Tristan, don't think you can just walk away from

me!" I hear a woman shout, and it gets our attention as a woman runs past us and grabs onto the arm of a man. The man turns, looking down at her. He has a nasty-looking scar running down one side of his face, and messy, black hair that needs a cut. He has a leather jacket on, pierced eyebrows, and his lip has a ring in it. The woman also has black hair, and her waist is fairly thin; she's very beautiful.

"You don't get it, Tria; this, me, isn't anything to do with you," Tristan says, and she lets go of his arm.

"That's Allie's brother and the nurse who was looking after him," Izzy whispers to me.

"So when you're getting drunk in a bar at ten in the morning, I'm meant to walk past?" Tria asks.

"Yes. What's so wrong with that?" Tristan replies.

"Tristan, everything is wrong with that," she says, and he laughs.

"Leave me alone, Tria. Face the fact that you can't fix me and move on. I don't want to be fixed," he says, storming off and disappearing into the crowd. Tria stands watching him before turning and walking away.

"I'm guessing that Tris got a lot closer to his nurse than he told Allie."

"Are you going to say something?"

"No. Allie told me Tristan has given up on life. He

doesn't care about anything anymore, but what I just saw—"

"Is a man who cares about someone, I agree," I say, there was no missing the way he looked at her, even despite what he said.

"Let's hope Tria doesn't give up."

"I don't think she will, she didn't seem to be giving up on Tristan at all," I comment, and Izzy smiles, hooking her arm in mine.

"Should we tell Harley about how you might have seen Daniel?"

"No, not with the fight so close, and I bet it's not even him. I just didn't sleep much last night; in fact, I haven't slept well for weeks. It's just stress messing with my head," I reassure her as I can't be sure it was him.

## CHAPTER 20
TILLY

"You're kissing me, then leaving," I mutter as Harley kisses me gently and steps back. I don't want to make him feel guilty, but as my hands tighten on his shirt, I know I don't want to let him go. I don't want him to stop kissing me.

"You know I have to do this. I will be back for you later. Look after our girl," he tells me, and I shake my head as I force myself to let go.

I hear Luke open the front door and walk out and, for some reason, that makes this all real to me. I've tried my best to get my head away from maybe seeing Daniel on the same day that Harley is going to walk into this fight.

"You can't promise me that, it's impossible for you to promise me anything right now," I say, and he sighs.

"Tilly."

"Just come back because . . ." I go to say the words I've only thought, but they get stuck in my throat just as Sebastian and Elliot come into the room.

"Have a good girls' night," Sebastian says to me, referring to Maisy, Allie, Izzy, and Emilia, who are waiting for me in the lounge.

They have already said their goodbyes to Harley and the others. The guys decided they all need to be at The Cage tonight. Except for Blake, who had to deal with Tristan tonight and didn't want to upset Allie with how Tristan is at the moment. Izzy told Blake to just try to help, and he has been, but it's, apparently, far more complicated than we knew.

"I will," I reply, faking a smile as they all walk out.

Harley stops at the door and looks at me. "I feel the same if that's anything. I have to say it before I leave," he tells me, and I smile.

"Me, too." I sigh, watching as his eyes light up, but then he nods, leaving and shutting the door behind him.

I go back into the lounge, where the girls are sitting across all the sofas eating various foods. Emilia has a gap next to her, and I go and sit down. Jake and my baby girl are sleeping upstairs in the cots we have, and Maisy has a baby monitor in her hand. It was so cute to see Jake come over and try to give baby girl one of his toys, and then he stayed next to her until she fell asleep.

"How long until your baby girl comes?" Emilia asks Maisy as Izzy puts in the DVD we have chosen for tonight. I don't know the movie, but it's something about bridesmaids.

"I'm due in for a section tomorrow," she says, and I can't believe how excited she must be. It's awesome that our babies are going to be so close in age. That they will grow up together and go to the same schools around here. Hopefully, they will be friends.

"Are you nervous?" Allie asks gently.

"Nope. I've done this once before, and yeah, I can't think about being nervous right now," she says, and we all settle down to watch the movie. The movie is funny and opens with a bad sex scene.

It has us all laughing within moments when Allie says, "That is not how Elliot–"

"Allie, don't," Izzy says, putting her hands on her ears.

I sit eating popcorn and drinking Coke as we watch the rest of the movie. My mind running over and over what Harley is about to do, and I know I can't stop him. I can't even be there for him.

"Guys," Maisy says, and Izzy pauses the movie.

"Yeah, you okay?" Izzy asks, and we go silent.

"My waters just went, and I need a section. I can't

have this baby naturally after what happened with Jake–" Maisy says in a nervous tone, and we all quickly get up. Someone turns the lights on as I help Maisy up, and Allie is on her other side. Maisy's leggings are soaked, and so is the sofa.

"Any contractions?" Allie asks Maisy, who shakes her head.

"Only one little one, nothing serious and nothing like how quick they came on last time," she says, holding her side.

"In my car, and you call Seb," Allie tells Izzy, who nods. She rings his phone several times as we get Maisy into the car.

"Is he coming?" Maisy asks Allie as she goes to shut the door.

"He will be there," I tell her gently, and she nods.

"He isn't answering, I bet he can't hear it over the music of The Cage," Izzy says once Allie shuts the door.

There is only one thing we can do; one of us needs to get to The Cage.

"Okay, I will drive there. Does anyone have the directions?" I ask, and they all look at each other.

"I will drive Maisy to the hospital, and you get Seb there now. No matter what," Allie says, and we all nod at her as she goes and gets into the car.

We watch her drive off before Emilia says, "I

know how to get there but can't drive as I've had a drink."

"Then I will drive. Izzy will stay and look after the kids," I say, and Izzy nods her agreement. I know she doesn't want to go near The Cage, and I don't blame her.

I look down at my leggings and long, red top and have no idea what the dress code is for The Cage. I look at Emilia in her black hoodie and black jeans, knowing that it can't be too dressy.

"I need to grab my jacket," I say, heading into the house. I find my leather jacket, pull it on, and grab my keys.

Izzy walks past me, still trying to call one of the guys, and I hope she gets through to one of them in time. She stops and grabs my arm to stop me from walking away.

"I will keep ringing, but Harley won't be happy to see you there. Be careful," Izzy tells me, letting go.

I don't have to say anything to her as I turn and walk toward the car.

"How do you know how to get there?" I ask Emilia as she gets into Harley's spare Range Rover. The car is perfect and new, making me think it isn't a spare like Harley said it was when he let me borrow it.

"My dad, he works there and so does the rest of

my family. It's a long story, but I've always known about The Cage," she says quietly.

"What do they do there?" I ask.

"Jobs for Arthur mainly, and even I work for him from time to time."

"What do you do for Arthur?" I ask her, hoping it's nothing to do with the brothers because I would never be able to forgive her if it was.

"Dancing, I pole dance for his clients sometimes. My mother does it, too, and it's something I don't have much of a choice in," she tells me, her hands tightening on her seats.

"Do the brothers know that?" I ask, wondering if they know Emilia is close to The Cage.

"No . . . Well, Luke does, but I would like it if you didn't say anything to the others," she tells me.

"I'm your friend, I'm not saying a word," I comment, and she smiles at me.

I pull the car out of their long drive and listen to Emilia's directions to The Cage. I'm surprised that it isn't that far away from town; it's in the middle of a deserted road. The empty road pulls out into a packed carpark and a massive warehouse sits the back of it.

"This doesn't look like The Cage," I say, commenting on how I expected it to be different.

"Make no mistake, Tilly, this place is as rough as it

looks, and I need to be honest with you, you need to be quiet in there and let me speak," she tells me.

I watch in shock as she pulls her hoodie off, revealing the tattoos lining her arms and the small tank top she's wearing that shows off her flat stomach. She pulls her hair down and runs her fingers through it.

"I can't go in there looking like I want to. Not worth the hassle Arthur or my family would give me if a client saw me. They expect me to be their wet dream and to pay thousands for a dance," she says, and her words are bitter.

"Do you ever sleep with them?" I ask her gently, and she shakes her head.

"Arthur sells the fact I'm a virgin to them, and I'm not to be touched. I know he will eventually sell me off to someone, but I plan to escape this hellhole of a town before that happens."

"Virgin?"

"That's what he thinks. There was this one night, with a guy who was amazing. But this is who I am. My family needs me, and whatever I feel can't get in the way of that," she tells me and then gets out of the car.

I follow her out and lock the car before walking up the path in the middle leading to the doors of the warehouse.

"Sis," one of the massive bouncers at the door says when he sees Emilia. The bouncer has a bald head, tanned skin similar to Emilia's, and dark hair. The other bouncer doesn't say a word as he continues to stare at me in the carpark.

"Hey, bro, I came to see the fight. Finally, there's a chance one of the famous King brothers is going to die, huh?" Emilia says, and I glare at her. What the hell?

"Damn straight. I've seen the people the boss chose for Harley. Wants him dead, all right," her brother says, and I hold the urge to hit one of them as they both laugh.

"Anyway, my friend here hasn't seen a fight before, and if she is going to see any, it's got to be tonight," Emilia says, hooking her arm through mine as the guy looks me up and down.

"Best show her what it's like then, and maybe bring her downstairs after if she needs some work." Her brother laughs and opens the door. I don't want to know what kind of work her brother just offered me, and I have no intention of ever finding out. I just need to find Harley. Emilia leads me in, and we walk down the steps to the entrance.

Once the door shuts, she whispers to me. "You have to act a certain way here or you don't make it. My brothers aren't like that behind closed doors, but here, it's different. If people aren't scared of you, then you shouldn't be here or you will be dead."

I don't get a chance to respond to her as she pushes the doors open to a massive room. The room is loud, the music blasting my ears, and the heat of the place makes me feel like I'm being swallowed whole. There's a massive cage in the middle, with bright lights shining on it. There are bars around the side and doors, leading off to god knows what on the sides.

I'm shocked at the number of people here. I didn't expect to see so many. Most of the women are wearing clothes that do little to hide their bodies, and the men are in tight suits. I don't know why I stop in my tracks as I take everything in, the smells of sweat and sweet perfumes fill my nose, and they make me want to run out the door.

"Come on!" Emilia shouts at me, just as I spot Harley.

Every part of me freezes when I see him, my mouth goes dry and fear fills me. He is in the cage, blood pouring down his face. Two men are unconscious at his feet, and he is facing three other guys. Two of them are massive, and the other looks like he shouldn't be in the fight at all.

There are hundreds of people around the cage, most shouting 'King,' but some are shouting other words I don't recognise. The noise is just that loud in here, but I can't move as I stare at Harley. I don't think I will ever forget seeing him this way, the way he looks dangerous, but I know straight away that this is not who he is.

Harley is the man who feeds my daughter when she wakes up at night, who brings me coffee in the morning. The man who cuts roses from plants in his garden and puts them in my bedroom window. The man I find asleep in his study with a new book in his hands. That's my Harley, and this is the man he has been forced to be for too long.

"I see Sebastian at the bar," she shouts at me, trying to pull my arm just as Harley rushes at two of the guys.

"Go, then," I say, unhooking my arm from hers and ignoring her when she tells me to come back. I push through the people and duck under others that are jumping up and down. It doesn't take me long to get to the front of the crowd, with my body pushed against the cage wall.

Harley is struggling to fight the guys as two of the huge ones hold him down and the other hits his side. I feel sick as I see the almost defeated look he is wearing; this fight isn't fair. He can't die like this, not after everything this hellhole has taken from him.

"HARLEY, FIGHT FOR ME!" I scream, just as his bright-green eyes find mine.

# CHAPTER 21
## HARLEY

"What happened this time?" I ask Elliot as I wait for the nurse to stitch up the cut on his back.

Our father called to tell me Elliot was here, but I don't know why he bothered to tell me as he doesn't usually give a fuck about the marks he has made. The cut on his back is thicker than the other one next to it, and the wad of cash sticking out from the nurse's pocket makes me realize my father has already paid her off. The more I look at her, the more I realise that she is one of the girls who hang around my father and Arthur a lot.

"I wouldn't fuck Hazel," he says quietly, and I tighten my fists. The nurse gives me a worried look, and I force myself to calm down.

"I'm going to deal with her," I tell Elliot, waiting for

*the nurse to finish up before leaving the hospital with Elliot.*

*"Don't bother. The girl is a fucking idiot," Elliot comments, and I shake my head as I open the car door for him.*

*"She needs to leave. I've had enough of our father using her to fuck with me, and now you. We deal with enough shit from him."*

*"She won't leave, she has no family to go to. Let's just go somewhere else, Harley. I don't want to go back there tonight," he tells me, and I look over at him. What little light there was in his eyes just seems to be disappearing by the day. Everything our father does drains him more, and I don't want Elliot to lose himself. Not when he is so young.*

*"Where do you want to go?"*

*"Don't know," he mutters, and I rest my hand on his shoulder.*

*"I do, let's get your brothers and go for a drink in the next town," I say, knowing I need to get him away from here.*

*"Sounds good," Elliot says, and some light comes back into his eyes.*

"You ready for this?" Elliot asks me as I finish wrapping my knuckles with tape, and I look over at him as the memory washes away.

Elliot looks far better than he did back then when everything was forced or taken from him. He finally has his girl, the one he always wanted, and he has everything to live for. I look down at the tape as I tie it. It's red, and it reminds me of Tilly's red hair. It makes me want to finish this quicker. Win this last fight and then get the hell out of here and back to my girl.

"Yes. Just . . . if I don't make it out of this, protect Tilly and her baby for me?" I ask him, knowing he is the only one out of my brothers who is being realistic.

Luke and Sebastian can't think of anything other than me walking out of here. But Elliot isn't like that. He knows how you have to fight for everything, and how I will be lucky to make it out of this fight in one piece. We always took the harder fights, the ones we knew would be hard to beat, but Luke and Sebastian don't know that. And they never will.

"Always," Elliot tells me, and that's all I need to hear as I stand up.

I've spent months working out for this, I'm stronger than I've ever been. I can do this, I've done it my whole life, but I've never fought more than three men at a time. I remember when I fought three when I turned eighteen; I just barely made it out of that fight then, but I'm a different man now. Years of fighting have made me tough, and I've never been in shape like I am today. I've spent weeks training for this moment, to get to where I need to be.

"I wish you would let me do this," Elliot comments, and I shake my head.

"No, this is my fight. Let me protect you now," I comment, and he pulls me into a hug. Elliot never hugs me, so I pat his back.

"Fucking beat those fuckers, and we can walk out of here. Then you can get your girl," he says as he lets go, and I nod.

Elliot walks out first, and then I follow, after pausing for a moment to collect my thoughts. I have to blank my mind for this fight, focus on nothing other than winning like I do every time. The screaming is blasting my ears from the number of people here, and the heat of The Cage is the hardest thing to block out.

There are far more spectators than there usually are for a fight, and Arthur looks happy as he stands outside the door to the cage. I don't look at him as I size up my opponents in the cage instead. There are five of them, three of them are massive, just like I expected, and I would reckon they are brothers with their similar looks and evil smirks. The next two are a little confusing as to why they are here. One looks like an almost nerdy guy, with a thin frame. I bet he moves fast. The last guy is blond with a pretty face that is not going to look good with bruises. I don't take any of their looks for face value, they must have some hidden qualities or tricks and that's why they are here. Arthur wouldn't let them into the fight if there wasn't a reason.

"Fight well," Arthur says when I get to him and stop.

"When I win this, I don't want to see your fucking face again," I spit out at him, and he snickers.

"I have a gift for you . . . if you win this," he says, smoothing down his suit.

"Why the fuck would you give me anything, Arthur?" I ask him, wondering what the fuck he is going on about. I don't need him messing with me just before a fight.

"I stand to make millions if you win. The number of bets against you are through the roof, but then . . ." He leans closer. "They don't know you like I do. They don't know you have a pretty baby and girl at home to win for," he whispers the end part, and I barely catch his words.

"Don't fucking talk about them, Arthur," I tell him, stepping closer and resisting the urge to slam him into that cage and beat the shit out of him.

"Don't let me down, Harley, like every single one of your deadbeat family has. I don't want anything to do with any of you anymore, and the money from this fight means I won't have to," Arthur says, stepping away.

"What is the gift? Why the fuck would I want anything from you?" I ask him, and he laughs as he walks off into the crowd. Fucking Arthur, messing with my head before a fight.

I walk into the cage, shutting the door behind me and hearing the crowd scream my name as I stand in front of the guys, who no doubt are being paid a fortune to win this fight. Or Arthur has something on them. Either way, I have to look out for my family and myself now.

"Pretty boy, why are you here?" I ask as the overhead speakers start counting down.

"You'll see. You can't always win." He laughs, and they all look at each other.

I crack my knuckles as I wait for the countdown to hit one. I think they expected me to run at them, and it seems to confuse them when I don't move.

"Come on, then," I say as I wave my hand at them, and they look between each other before one of the big guys runs forward, with the pretty guy following. I catch the man in a headlock, surprised how stupid he was to lower his head, and then lift my knee, slamming it into his chest. I spin away from the guy as he falls to his knees, and the blond man comes toward me. I have to give it to him, he is a good fighter, but it only takes me a few moments to punch him in the face as hard as I can, and he is out cold. The blood from his broken nose squirts all over my face.

"Is that the best you have?" I laugh at them.

The two guys grin at me together, this time getting several hits on my body before I manage to spin away from them both. The thin guy takes me by surprise when he slams a punch into my stomach and then jumps over me. The shock of the thin man attacking is all the other two need as they grab both my arms. The thin man walks in front of me and smirks.

"I trained for years to kill you. I doubt you remember my brother, he is in a coma because of you," the thin man says, all the nervous acting he was doing before is gone. He lifts his hand and punches me, punch after punch until I can't hold my head up. I don't remember his brother, I don't remember any of the men I fight. I had to put every man I fought in the back of my mind, forgetting they ever happened.

"HARLEY FIGHT FOR ME!" I hear Tilly's voice shout through the haze.

I lift my head, my eyes locking on her as she hangs onto the bars of the cage. What the fuck is she doing here?

"Tilly," I whisper, and then, the man punches me once more.

Thoughts of Tilly run through my head as I roar and push the men holding me away with all of my strength. The man in front looks shocked, but he tries to punch me again, which is a big mistake for him as I catch his hand and crush it in my own. I use my other hand to lift the thin man close to my face as he screams for me to let go of his hand.

"I'm sorry about your brother, and this," I tell him, and his eyes widen just before I let go of his hand and punch him hard in the face. I'm not shocked when he falls to the ground as I let him go before I turn to face the two large guys waiting for me.

"I haven't got all the time in the world . . ." I laugh, waiting for them to run at me as the screaming of the crowd gets louder.

I wipe the blood off my lip as I smile at them. They look at each other and then somehow seem to decide that running at me together is the best way. It's a bad move on their part. I grab the one who gets to me first, punching his head and roundhouse kicking him in the side. He falls into the other guy, and they both fall to the ground. I jump on him as he flies over his friend, and I start punching his face. He is out cold in two minutes. The other guy gives me a panicked look when I pull his friend's unconscious body off him.

"Don't," the man says, holding up his hands as he backs away. The sight of all the unconscious men at my feet has freaked him out, and he isn't going to try to attack me, not now.

"You shouldn't have come here," I say, slamming my fist into his face, and he stumbles backward. I grab his head, slamming it into the bars of the cage and kicking his legs as he falls to the ground.

"THE KINGS HAVE WON!" cheers a voice over the speakers, and the crowd screams.

My eyes meet Tilly's just as Luke gets to her side and gives me a nod. He will keep her safe in here. I walk out of the cage, where Arthur is waiting. He offers me a towel, and I just look at him.

"Don't you like seeing me covered in blood? It's how you make your money." I laugh, and he narrows his eyes at me. I wipe some of the blood off my face and slap his face, leaving blood all over him.

"Take it, and get out," he says, pulling out a note from his pocket and giving it to me.

"Gladly," I take the note, walking away from the bastard and toward the changing rooms.

When the changing room doors are closed behind me, I rest my head on them. *I fucking won.*

## CHAPTER 22
### TILLY

"Here let me," I mutter as Harley tries to push the ice away that I'm holding to his lip.

He smiles at me before gently kissing me, and I sigh. Ever since he walked out of The Cage with Em at his side, he hasn't said he is in any pain at all when I know he must be. I waited as he came back and showered the blood off and got dressed. I offered him painkillers, but he refused to have any.

"It doesn't hurt," he says, and I give him a disbelieving glare. Harley's one eye is swollen, nearly shut, and there are a range of bruises already showing all over his face. I don't believe him for a second.

"You know how awesome you are? Allie says 'awesome' a lot and–" He sways a little in the seat.

"You fought five guys today, there's no way you're not in pain, and yes, Allie says 'awesome' a lot," I tell him and give him a worried look. What if he has a concussion or something?

"It's the painkillers I crushed into his drink," Luke says, sitting on the sofa with my baby girl in his arms, and I give him a wide-eyed look. "What? I knew the stubborn fucker wouldn't have them." He shrugs.

"Language," Harley says with a dopey smile as he leans back on the sofa. I watch as he slowly falls asleep, and I move him so that he is lying down on the sofa. I pull one of the blankets over him as Izzy comes into the room.

"It was a good idea; he needs to rest," I comment, stroking Harley's hair off his face and watching him for a second as Luke doesn't say a word.

"Any news on Maisy?" I ask.

"Is he all right?" Izzy asks, and I nod.

"Oh . . . no news. They are letting the labour go naturally, and she is close, apparently," she says, going to sit next to Luke. "Let me hold baby girl," Izzy says, and Luke shakes his head.

"Nope, I got her to sleep after she woke up, so I'm holding her," he says, and I smile at him. "A name yet?" Luke asks, and I shake my head.

"I have some time to decide," I mutter, and Izzy laughs.

"Come on, you must have some idea for a name," she tells me.

"Okay, there was this one name-" I get cut off when Izzy's phone starts buzzing, and she answers the call.

"Oh my god, congratulations, Seb, that's amazing. Yes, I will tell them. Love you, bro, and I will be at the hospital in the morning. Jake is fine, I promise. Bye," Izzy says all this so quickly that neither Luke nor I can say a word until she puts the phone down.

"A girl, she's perfect, and Maisy is doing well. They decided to call her Isabelle," Izzy says, and there are grins from all of us as we look at each other. Izzy's phone starts ringing and she moves quickly to answer it.

"It's Blake, he is at the hospital as he drove Seb and Elliot." She tells us before walking out.

"Here, pass her to me. I'm taking her back to bed, and I will check Jake before I go to sleep, myself," I say to Luke who offers me my baby girl, and I hold her close to my chest. I look down at her, seeing how her curly, red hair is growing already, and I love the little snores she makes as she sleeps. Harley makes a small, groaning noise, and I look over at him. I hate seeing him like this, in so much pain, but I'm happy it's over. This is the first and only time I will have to see him suffer like this.

"I'm watching him for the night," Luke tells me, seeing where I'm staring.

I look over at the youngest King brother. The tattoos he has lining his arms, the scruffy hair, and slight beard make him look older than all his brothers. I would say he is the more playful one out of them all, but there are still those shadows in his eyes. The same shadows they all have, but Harley has them the worst from what I know. His shadows are the most difficult to erase.

"I'm still going to check he is okay in a few hours, you don't have to stay up all night," I reply to Luke. I know I won't be able to sleep well tonight, knowing Harley isn't completely okay.

"He's my brother, there isn't anything I wouldn't do for him, and that includes watching movies on my phone down here until he wakes up in the morning," he says.

"He feels the same about you and all your brothers. I know because I've always been protective of my brothers, too," I say and mentally chuckle to myself about all the times I've helped them get out of trouble. There's something about having close siblings, it has a way of making you feel loved and knowing you have someone protecting your back.

"It's what Kings do, apparently Foxes are just the same," he says, and I wink at him.

"You have that right."

"Can I ask you something?" Luke asks, nervously moving on the sofa. I've never seen him nervous before.

"Sure," I say, sitting on the edge of the sofa and moving my baby onto my shoulder. I pat her back gently as she stirs a little. I'm lucky she loves her sleep and is happy whenever someone is holding her.

"Okay, so there's this girl . . ." he starts off, "that sounded more rehearsed than I wanted it to."

"I'm listening," I say with a little chuckle, and he groans.

"She is complicated as fuck, messes with my head, but I can't stop thinking about her. We had a one-night stand and afterward, she just . . . ."

"Just?"

"I don't know. Let's just say I know she is hiding something from me, but I don't know what it is. I can't figure her out, but no other girl compares to her. Nothing compares to her," Luke says, and I nod, looking at Harley.

"Then don't give up, no matter how messed-up things are, how hard they get, you fight. That's what your brother taught me, and it's what he would tell you if you asked him. If you can't stop thinking about her, there's a reason for that," I say, knowing that there's a reason I can't stop thinking about Harley.

"Thanks. Just . . . part of me wants to give up on her sometimes, but then even thinking of doing that . . . yeah, I can't," Luke says, looking down at his hands.

"Then she is worth it," I say gently, and he smiles up at me.

"Thanks, Tills," Luke smiles, looking down at his phone as he slips it in his hand.

"No problem. Night, Luke," I reply.

"Night." He waves a hand.

I gently shut the door behind me as I leave the room and go upstairs. When I get to my room, I put my baby in her cot and kiss her head. I check on Jake before getting into bed, and then I close my eyes, letting the small sound of my baby's little snores lure me to sleep.

"Tilly," I hear whispered gently, and I blink my eyes open to see Harley lying next to me on the bed, our faces inches apart. Harley doesn't look any better this morning, his eye is still swollen shut, and his face is a muted colour of bruises. His lip has a long cut on the left side, but the swelling has gone down a little.

"Harley?" I ask in a little bit of a daze.

"Shh, baby girl is still sleeping," Harley says, putting his finger to my lips. I look over my shoulder to see it's still dark outside, and I can see my baby sleeping in her cot.

"How are you feeling?" I ask Harley quietly, placing my hand on his chest.

"Better, although I'm not accepting drinks from Luke anymore. I should have known he would do that," he says, and I smile.

"I kind of like that he did, you needed your rest," I say, and he grins.

"Any news on Maisy and Isabelle?" I ask him, and he pulls his phone out of his jean pocket. I wait as he unlocks it and then shows me photos of Maisy and Sebastian holding a little baby with black hair. I look closer and see she looks just like Maisy and Jake. Jake and Isabelle have the same black hair. Above the photo is a message saying 'she has my green eyes,' and I know she is going to be the image of her brother.

"They look so happy," I say as I hand him his phone back, and he puts it in his jeans.

"They do," he says. I pause when he leans closer, our mouths only inches away from each other, and he reaches over, tucking some of my hair behind my ear.

"Tilly, I want a date on Friday. Five days away.

I've been planning it for a while," he says, and I love that he has been planning a date for us. For the future we can now have.

"We go on dates already," I whisper back, and he chuckles.

"Nothing like this one. This one is the start of us, Tilly. You'd best be ready," he teases me.

"So should you, Mr. King," I whisper back and brush my lips against his.

He responds by kissing me again harder, an almost desperate kiss as he rolls himself over me. The sound of the baby crying only moments later makes us break apart. "Friday, Tilly," Harley says, getting off of me and standing up and walking over to my baby. He picks her up, and she instantly stops crying.

"I can sort her, you only just had that fight and I know you must be sore," I comment, but he kisses her forehead and rests her in his arms.

"Let me, please. Everyone in this room is what I survived for," he tells me, and I nod, emotion filling me. "I'm going to feed her some milk while you wake up."

"Trust me, every part of me is awake," I mutter, and he grins at me before walking out.

# CHAPTER 23
## HARLEY

"What did you say?" I repeat to the doctor, trying to sit up, but Elliot puts a hand on my chest, making me lie back down.

The strong smell of medicine and the ticking of the heart monitor are annoying me as I try to process what he is telling me. Every part of my body hurts as I try to sit up, my voice croaks from my dry throat.

"You just woke from a coma, a three-day fucking coma. Please rest," Elliot begs me, and I look at my fourteen-year-old brother and nod. I dread to know what our father has been putting him through in the last few days, but the bruises on his face tell me enough. I hate being away from them, not there to take the hits and divert my father's attention.

"You cannot have children, Mr. King. The operation

*we had to do . . ."* *he keeps talking, but I don't hear anything else he says.*

*I knew it was bad when the man I was fighting pulled that knife out and stabbed me, right under my cock. I knew when I punched him and he passed out that my brothers would get me to the hospital, that the damage would be severe. But I never expected this.*

*"Mr. King, are you listening to me?"* *the doctor asks, and I ignore him as the door opens.*

*Luke and Sebastian walk in, bruises on their faces, and I know that I might never be able to have children, but my brothers need my protection now. There are worse things that can happen in life, and I could always adopt a child who has shitty parents like mine one day.*

*"I heard you and I understand. Now leave, I want to talk to my brothers,"* *I tell the doctor, who gives me a worried look but walks out.*

*"Harley–"* *Elliot starts to say, and I shake my head at him. I don't want anyone else to know. As far as I'm concerned, I already have a family who needs me.*

"Impressive." Luke whistles when I walk into the kitchen in my tuxedo.

"Do I look all right?" I ask him, worrying about my hair, which I've spent ages on, braiding the sides back. The tuxedo is tight but made to fit, so I have to think it looks good.

"Yeah, man, but don't worry. That girl loves you

anyway," he says, walking past me and patting my shoulder. When did my youngest brother get so grown up?

"Fucking hell," I whisper to myself when I see Tilly walk into the corridor wearing a tight, black dress that Allie helped me choose for her. The dress is simple, just black, but the long slit up to her thigh just makes her look stunning. Her red hair is half up in a bun, and the rest falls down her back in curls.

"Harley?" she calls, like the damn siren she is. I find myself helpless in doing anything but walking straight over to her. Her eyes widen when she sees me and I can't help but grin.

"You look so beautiful, Tilly," I tell her, not knowing what else to say to her. 'Beautiful' doesn't even seem like a strong enough word to describe how she looks. She is just something else.

"Thank you, and thank you for the dress. How did you know my size?" she asks, but it's Allie who answers for me.

"He called me, and I knew your size from one look," she says as she walks out of the lounge with Elliot at her side. Allie has the baby monitor in her hand, and she offered to babysit baby girl tonight so I can take Tilly out. Elliot was just dragged along, but he doesn't seem too bothered.

"Are you sure about having her all night?" Tilly asks Allie. Allie comes over and hugs her gently.

"Positive, now go. If we have any trouble, I will call. You both deserve a night out," Allie tells her, and she nods.

"I'm here, too, and baby girl loves me," Luke comments, leaning against the wall.

"Only because you keep watching Minions with her." Tilly laughs.

"It's a funny film." Luke shrugs and walks off.

"Let's go," I say to Tilly and take her hand in mine.

We walk out to my car, and I hold the door open. Tilly goes to get in and then changes her mind, turning and leaning up to kiss me gently and making me smile before she turns and gets in. After I get in, we start the ten-minute drive to the place I want to take her.

"Where are you taking me then?" she asks.

"We have to take another means of transport to get there first," I tell her, just as I pull into the drive of the house I was looking for. I drive down and park outside the giant house, and Tilly gives me a questioning look.

"Trust me?" I ask her, and she laughs.

"More than I want to admit," she says and then gets out the car. I get out and walk around the car, wrapping my arms around her waist as we walk to the front door. The door opens before we can press the doorbell.

"Harley, you all ready?" Mark asks me as he comes out of the house and shakes my hand.

"Yes, and thank you for doing this for me," I tell him.

"Don't thank me, I owe you anyway." Mark waves a hand. "Let's go get into the helicopter. My pilot is ready," he says.

Mark is a good man who used to fight in The Cage and couldn't pay back the debt he owed Arthur. A debt he owed Arthur for the lifesaving treatment his daughter needed and the transport to America as they couldn't save her here. That was years ago when I was eighteen, and he wasn't rich. I paid the debt off for him from my savings because I knew he would end up getting himself killed in The Cage; Mark isn't a fighter. Mark then took his freedom and set up a very successful truck driving business. He paid me back the money two years ago and insisted on helping me however he could. This is the first thing I've asked of him because he is the only one I know who has a helicopter.

"Helicopter?" Tilly gives me a wide-eyed look, and I grin at her. I'm sure she can hear it from here, the noise is loud.

"Yes. The helicopter is going to take us to our date," I say, and she chuckles.

"Always surprising me with dates I will never forget," she says.

"I never want you to forget me," I whisper into her ear as I wrap my arm around her shoulders while we walk toward the helicopter.

"I could never forget you, Harley King," she tells me, having to basically shout it for me to hear as we get closer to the helicopter.

We lower our heads as we get into the helicopter as it's already on. After we all have our earphones in and our seatbelts strapped on, the helicopter takes off and Tilly squeezes my hand tight in hers.

"It's amazing up here," Tilly comments as we fly across the countryside and toward London, where we are staying for the night.

I had bags with some clothes sent there yesterday, and everything we need to stay the night is already waiting for us. I know the flight is only forty-five minutes to get into London. Tilly comments about all the beautiful views there are; the city lights, the towns. All I can think of is how beautiful she is. I spend the whole trip watching her, the way her eyes widen and the happy smile she gives me sometimes.

"Landing," I hear in our headphones from Mark, and the pilot nods.

"Thank you for this, it's just amazing," Tilly tells me, leaning into my side as the helicopter lands. We have to keep our heads low as we move away from the helicopter, and we watch from the door as Mark and the pilot fly away.

"London?" she asks me as she looks around the view of the city from the rooftop we are standing on.

"Have you ever been?"

"No, I've always wanted to see it."

"Well, after tonight, we can spend the morning looking around the tourist parts before we have to fly back. Your mum and dad are coming over to look after baby girl."

"I would love that. You have planned everything, haven't you?" she asks, and I chuckle.

"I've been planning this date for months, from the first time I kissed you," I tell her, and she tilts her head to the side.

"Mr. King?" a man asks from the door to the roof, and I take Tilly's hand in mine as we walk over.

"Yes, and this is Miss Fox," I say, introducing Tilly while shaking his hand.

"I'm your driver to the theatre tonight, and I will drive you to the hotel afterward," he tells her, as I already know this.

"Thank you," Tilly responds.

"We should be going; the show starts in an hour,

and the traffic is difficult to get through at this time of night. There are refreshments in the limo," he tells us.

"Theatre, limo, and a hotel in London?" Tilly whispers as the man opens the door and we follow him to the lift. We wait for the lift to come up after he presses the button.

"You're worth every second of it," I whisper back, sliding my fingers up her spine and making her shiver.

"I don't need fancy things, Harley, I only need you," she whispers back, and I lean down, kissing her gently.

"I know, but I want this for you. Trust me," I tell her gently, and she kisses me once more before leaning away. I keep my hand in the middle of her back, not ready to let her step away from me yet.

"Always," she says, and the lift beeps as it opens. I find myself struggling to look away from her eyes.

"Mr. King?" the man says, and Tilly walks forward into the lift, with me following.

The lift opens up into the entrance hall of the hotel we will be staying at later. We go outside to the limo parked, waiting for us, and the man opens the door. Tilly gets in, and I follow her, waiting for the door to be shut.

"What are we seeing at the theatre?" she asks.

"You remember when I brought roses to your room, and you told me that story about your favourite, childhood story?" I remind her.

"The Princess and the Pea?" she asks in a whisper.

"Well, I found this theatre performance and knew you might like it," I tell her, watching as her eyes light up, and she has the biggest smile on her face.

"Oh my god. I've wanted to see this performance since it was advertised, but the tickets were impossible to get a hold of unless you pay . . ." her voice drifts off.

"It took about a week to find tickets but you're worth it," I say, and she blushes as she looks down.

"I never thought I'd see the day when your cheeks match your hair," I say, and she gently hits me on the arm.

"This is the most romantic thing anyone has ever done for me, Harley," she says gently, and I pick her hand up, kissing the back as gently as her words.

"Then every man before me was an idiot. You should have always been treated like this, and if you let me . . . I want to be yours. I never wanted anything serious before I met you, I didn't even think of it as an option. But then you stormed into my life, and I can't imagine my life without you in it. I'm a messed-up man, with a bad past, but I swear I will do anything to give you a perfect future," I tell her, and her breath catches as a stray tear falls from her eyes. I wipe it away, and she leans her head into my hand.

"I don't need a perfect future, but I need you at my side; only you, Harley," she says, and then I lean down and kiss her. The kiss is broken when the limo stops and the door opens a few moments later.

"Wait," Tilly says when I go to get out.

"Yeah?" I ask, and she chuckles as she wipes something from the side of my lip.

"My lipstick," she says, and I kiss her.

"Don't care," I say, getting out of the car as I hear her laugh behind me.

I link my arm around her waist as we walk into the theatre, following the red rug on the floor. The theatre is amazing inside, everything is gold. Gold walls and floors, gold statues lining the walls. Our driver speaks to the staff, and then he takes us into the room we rented on the top floor overlooking the play. I open the door and thank the driver for shutting it behind me. There is a row of seats near the balcony and a buffet filled with food and drinks on the side. There is a small, white table, with two chairs set up in the other corner of the room. There's light music playing from the theatre stage, and Tilly goes to look over the balcony.

"Is this all ours? The view is amazing," Tilly says, and I move to stand next to her, pushing her hair to the side and gently kissing down her neck.

"Yes, it's all ours for the night," I say, and her breath catches when I gently suck on the spot under her ear. She turns in my arms, looking up at me and not moving as we stare at each other.

"Can anyone see us here?" she asks, sliding her hands down my chest. I know we are at the highest point.

"Not if we move further back into the room," I say with a smirk, and she leans up and kisses me.

I want to take it slow, as I enjoy how she tastes, how her soft lips move across mine, but when she slides her hands into my hair, I can't control the kiss anymore. The kiss becomes frantic from both of us, a kiss built up from all the tension we have had with each other since we first met. I walk backward, keeping my hands in her hair, and move her closer to the table in the room. I lift her onto the table as her hands slide down my waist and start undoing my trousers. I pull her dress down her chest, exposing her perfect breasts, and lean forward, twirling my tongue around one and making her moan louder.

"Shhh," I say, and she chuckles a little for a second, but then she pushes down my trousers and boxers, pulling my hard cock into her soft hand. She moves her hand up and down, making me groan with how amazing it feels.

"Tilly," I bite out, pushing her dress up to her hips and seeing her lack of underwear.

"You're a bad girl, aren't you?" I ask her, just before sliding my finger inside her and feeling how wet she is.

I rub my thumb around her clit, loving her little moans and the way her hand strokes my cock harder. When I feel her getting tighter around my finger, and her moans getting to the point where I know she is close to coming on my hand, I pull my finger out. I grab her hips and line my cock up before kissing her and sliding inside. She moans into my mouth, her nails pressing into my neck as I thrust into her again and again.

"Harley, oh my god, don't stop." She moans again and again as I feel her tighten around me and I pick up speed. I finish only moments later, our heavy breathing and her moans still filling the room.

"I love you, Harley King," she tells me, and I gently lean forward, kissing her.

"I love you, too, Tilly Fox."

## CHAPTER 24
TILLY

"TILLY!" I hear Izzy shout up the stairs just as I put baby girl down for her nap after a feed.

I cringe and look down at baby girl, praying that she doesn't wake up, but she only stirs a little before rolling onto her side and cuddling the dinosaur teddy Jake gave her. I bought her lots of pink teddies and dolls, yet the old dinosaur teddy is what she has to sleep with every time.

I lean down and kiss her forehead, loving the little smile she gives, even in her sleep. She is so cute. I pick the baby monitor up and shut the bedroom door quietly just as Izzy gets to the top of the stairs and runs over to me.

"I'm engaged!" she says, showing me her hand with the large engagement ring on her finger. The ring has a large diamond in the middle and sapphires on the sides. I know Izzy has a sapphire necklace, and that it's the only thing she has left from her mother; the fact he put those in the engagement ring is so sweet.

"Oh my god! I'm so happy for you!" I say, pulling her hand up and looking at the stunning ring closely.

"You have to tell me everything, the when and the where. Come on." I tug on her hand and lead her up the stairs to Harley's attic room, knowing he is out at the gym this morning. We both go and sit on the sofa, and she starts off.

"Okay, you know all the trips he took me on?" I nod. "Well, he has been trying to propose to me at each one, but something was always going wrong."

"Okay, I feel really sorry for Blake now." I chuckle, and she laughs.

"I know, right?" She looks down at her ring and then back up at me. "So, last night, we stayed at his mum's and had dinner. It was great, but some nurses had called in sick so his mum had to go in to cover. Then we had a power cut, and the power was out all night."

"Same here, it must have been a blackout," I tell her, and she nods.

"So, imagine this, the living room full of candles,

the fire in the fireplace lit, and we were lying on the rug, after doing stuff–"

"To keep warm?" I wiggle my eyebrows at her, and she laughs.

"Exactly." She winks. "Anyway, Blake went into the kitchen to get more candles, as some had gone out, and his phone started ringing. I went and grabbed his jacket to find his phone, just in case it was important–"

"And you found the ring box?" I say, clapping my hands.

"Well, it fell out onto the floor and I picked it up, opening it as Blake came in. He laughed, explaining all the romantic things he had planned and how they all went wrong as he held my one hand and got down on one knee."

"Aww," I say, wiping my eyes. This is exactly what I wanted for her; she deserves this so much.

"The speech he gave me, about how we met, the struggles we had, and how he never wants me anywhere but at his side . . . oh my god, I was in tears," Izzy says, wiping a few tears away at the memory.

"You remember when we used to sit and watch those witch TV shows with your mum? How she told you that you'd find a perfect guy one day," I say, and she chuckles.

"I remember we used to watch those shows over and over again." She sniffles a little. "I miss her. I wish she was here to help me pick a dress, and to meet Blake," Izzy admits.

"She would have loved him," I say, squeezing her hand.

"I know. Would you be my maid of honour?" she asks me suddenly, and I pull her to me. I wrap my arms around her, and she sobs a little into my shoulder.

"Of course, I will, and even though your mum isn't here, we won't forget her on your wedding day. She will be with you," I tell her, rubbing her back.

"I know she is with me. I see her when I do simple things like buying apples from the shops and how she used to pick each one up and see what shape they were before buying them."

"I remember she didn't like apples that were odd shapes." I chuckle with Izzy as I pull away from the hug.

"Thank you for coming here, I didn't realise how much I missed having someone from my past around until you came here. I know I could talk about my mum to anyone, but it's not the same. I know you remember her."

"I'm always here to talk," I tell her, and she holds my hand.

"I'm going to ask Harley to walk me down the aisle, and I know Blake is asking Sebastian to be his best man," she tells me. "Right . . . I have to go tell Allie and Maisy. We are meeting up for lunch. Do you want to come?" she asks me.

"No, hun. I have work to catch up with. But have fun," I say, hugging her once more before she leaves.

I pull my laptop off the coffee table and start editing the book that was sent to me yesterday. Thankfully, the author is in no rush, but I don't want to leave her long without getting the first edit back to her. I spend the next half an hour editing. I know I can't do too much more before baby girl wakes up.

"Hey, gorgeous," I hear Harley say as he comes into the room and shuts the door. I put my laptop down, knowing I will have to do more tonight. Overall, it's not badly written, and it won't be a massive job.

"Hey, did you hear about Izzy and Blake?" I ask, watching as he comes over and sits next to me on the sofa. Harley looks so much more relaxed and less stressed since everything with Arthur is behind him and we are together. I like seeing him like this, and the smile he always wears.

"Yeah, she called. Thank God, he actually managed to ask without something going wrong. I was starting to feel bad for him." Harley chuckles, and I move across the sofa, swinging my one leg over him and sitting on his lap.

"I missed waking up next to you this morning," I whisper across his lips.

"I gave you a lie in, you deserved it." He chuckles, and I brush my lips down his neck, his hands tightening on my hips. "Tilly," he warns when I move my hips and rub myself against him, feeling him getting hard beneath me.

"Yes, Harley?" I ask, sliding off his lap and onto my knees in front of him.

I slowly undo his belt as he watches me, his eyes locked on mine the whole time. He lifts his hips a little to help me pull his trousers off, and I take his large cock into my hand. He groans as I lean forward, sliding my tongue around the tip before gently sucking him into my mouth. He is big enough that it's hard not to gag when I take all of him into my mouth, and he grabs my hair, holding my head in place as I keep still, letting him take over. He fucks my mouth, hard and fast as it's clear he is losing control, but I love it. I love seeing him relax like this. He suddenly stops, lifting me up, and pushing me onto the sofa. I moan a little when he pulls my leggings and red panties off before turning me so that I'm on my knees on the sofa. I feel his hand cup me from behind.

"So wet from just having me in your mouth," he whispers, more to himself, before he moves his hand and slides his cock deep inside me.

I arch my back as he grabs my hips and starts pounding away, his grip almost bruising, but the pleasure of having him inside me makes me barely notice. My own hand slides down, rubbing circles on my clit and if anything, it makes him lose more control as he moves faster inside me. He leans forward just as I come and bites down on my shoulder gently, and I moan his name as he finishes inside me. I collapse to the sofa with Harley pulling me to him so that I'm lying on his chest.

"It's never been like this," he says after a long silence.

"Like what?" I ask him.

"It's never meant anything to me, it was just sex. With you, I swear I feel everything, and I never want it to end," he says.

"It will never end, I don't want it to either," I whisper, and he holds me tighter.

## CHAPTER 25

TILLY

"Hey, you," I say, resting my hand on Harley's back, and he turns around with a smile. I rake my eyes over him, seeing him covered in dirt from the gardening he has been doing all day. It's been three days since the theatre. As soon as we got back, Harley moved my baby and me into his bedroom. He had already emptied a wardrobe for us. My eyes can't move away from the muscled body under his shirt, the way his hair is down like it always is when he gardens, and, finally, to meet his amused, green eyes.

"What exactly are you thinking about?" he asks, and I grin.

"Wouldn't you like to know?" I reply.

"I'm nearly finished here, and then I will have a

shower and cook if you want? Maybe we can do whatever you were just thinking about?" he asks me.

"I can cook," I tell him, and he nods, reaching out his dirt-covered hands to hold me.

"Err, nope. You are all dirty," I say, making him chuckle.

"But I want a dirty kiss from my girlfriend," he says, standing up as I walk backward. When I see the playful look in his eyes, I turn and run into the house, hearing him laughing behind me all the way.

I stop running when I get to the kitchen and put the baby monitor down on the side as baby girl sleeps. I've booked to register her birth in three days, and I still haven't chosen a name. I don't know why it seems so hard to do. I have a list of names, but none of them seem to suit her.

I put some pasta on to boil and then get the ingredients out to make the cheese sauce. I'm grating cheese when my phone rings, and I pick up.

"Hello?" I ask, but no one answers. I look down at the number, seeing it's unknown. *I keep getting these phones calls this week.*

"Hello?" I ask again. Still no reply.

The phone goes dead, and I put it on the side. I doubt it's anything other than someone selling something, or a dodgy line. I grate the cheese and add it to the sauce I've made as Harley comes into the kitchen.

Harley's hair is still slightly wet, hanging around his handsome face, and he only has a pair of black, jogging trousers on, showing off his impressive chest.

"I checked baby girl, and she is fast asleep. What are you making?" he asks, coming over and sliding his hands around my waist.

"Cheese pasta," I comment, as he kisses my cheek. "It's going to be a little while yet," I tell him, turning off the heat. I drain the pasta, while Harley watches, and mix it in with the sauce. I add it to a tray and put more grated cheese on top before placing the tray into the oven.

"Can I ask you to do something with me?" Harley asks me, and I turn to look at him after closing the oven.

"What's up?" I ask. I know him well enough to see he is worried about something.

"Arthur gave me this note after I won the fights. It's only an address, time, date, and a name I don't recognise," he says, handing the note to me. The address isn't far from here, about forty minutes away, and the name 'Julie Smith' is written above it. At the bottom is tomorrow's date and a time: two thirty.

"I Google searched the address, it's a home for mentally ill people, a dodgy one at that," Harley says with a confused look that matches mine.

"Why would he send you there?" I ask, having no clue what to make of it.

"That's the point, I don't know," he says, and I hand the note back to him.

"Of course I will go with you. I will ask my mum to come and sit with baby girl," I comment, and he nods.

"Thank you, I doubt it's anything, but I want you at my side either way," he tells me, and I lean up, kissing his cheek.

"Are you registering the baby's name as baby girl?" he asks with a cheeky grin.

"No," I say, chuckling.

"Okay, how about after we go to this tomorrow, we sit and go through names?" he asks, and I nod.

"I would love that," I say.

"Harley, does it bother you that I have a daughter? That . . . well–" I blurt out, and he puts a finger to my lips.

"Can I tell you the truth?" he asks me and even though part of me doesn't want to know, I still nod.

"A tiny part of me hates that she isn't my daughter, not biologically, anyway. Another part of me wants to be like a dad to her. I hope one day you might let me adopt her and marry you. I'm a hundred percent in this with you, and she comes with you. I'm not that kind of man, Tilly. I love you, and I love her, too," he tells me, his voice strong and firm. There isn't a part of me that doesn't doubt how he feels.

"Harley," I say with a sigh.

"You know I can't have kids. That I want to adopt someday; it's always been my plan. This was never my plan, but I'm a believer in fate. I think it's fate that brought both of you to me, and I plan to keep you both happy and safe," he tells me.

"Why don't you come with me when I register her? I will never let Daniel near her, and I know you're not her father, but you have been one to her since she was born. That means more," I say.

"You mean that? I could bring my lawyer and formally adopt her that way," he says, thinking about it.

"No one has to know she isn't yours, Harley, if you're on the birth certificate . . ." I say, and he nods.

"If this is what you want," he tells me, and I wrap my arms around him, resting my head against his chest.

"It is," I whisper.

"We will have to tell her someday, who her biological father really is and everything that happened. I don't want her to hate us if she finds out any other way."

"When she is older, we will tell her together," I agree.

I know I will have to tell my baby girl one day about her biological father, but she won't able to understand the reasons I ran away from him until she's older. I just hope he never finds us, not just for our sake, but for Harley's. I know Harley would kill him if he came anywhere near me.

# CHAPTER 26
## HARLEY

"You never tell us anything about our mother," I tell my father as he lies back on the sofa, looking up at the ceiling. I wouldn't dare ask him anything about our mother if he wasn't so drunk that he can't even stand up. I look at my pathetic excuse for a father, dribble coming out of his mouth and his dazed eyes. I doubt it's just alcohol in his system tonight.

"Your mother was smart and perfect for me to control," he mumbles out.

"Did you love her? Why did she leave?" I ask him, and he laughs.

"I never loved her, only one girl was for me and—" he goes to answer and falls to sleep, his body falling onto the sofa. I wonder who the girl he loved was, and I hope she is far away from this mess of a man. When I look at my father, it makes more sense why my mother left, but I will *never understand why she left us with him. What kind of mother would leave her children with a monster?*

"This place looks rough," Tilly says as I pull into the drive of the mental home. She must be thinking the same things as I am.

The place doesn't have a colour in sight, even the grass is dead, and the trees look like they are ill. The building is massive but looks like a reformed warehouse. There are gates to get into the driveway, and the building itself has moss growing all over it. Some of the windows look broken, and all of them have thick bars on the outside. There is a massive door with steps up to it, and I pull my car into the parking bay next to five other cars. I look over at Tilly, who I don't even want to bring into this place. It looks like something out of a horror film, and the online pictures must have been years old because they had flowers and the pavement wasn't cracked in them.

"You don't have to come in, I know this place looks dodgy as hell," I mutter, and she takes my hand as I turn the car off and pull the keys out.

"I'm in this with you, remember?" she says, and I lift her hand, kissing it gently before we get out of the car.

I wrap my arm around Tilly's waist as we walk up the steps, and I hold the door open for her. There is a big desk with stairs behind it, and several doors in the corridor. Everything is grey in here, much like the outside of the building. The woman behind the desk must be in her sixties, with long, grey hair and a nurse's uniform on, but she matches the décor, too.

"Can I help you?" she asks me, and I smooth my suit down before answering her.

"Is there someone named Julia Smith here?" I ask, and she nods.

"Ah, you're her visitor this week. Her frequent visitor told us you would be coming," she says, picking up the old-fashioned phone. It looks close to falling apart, like most of the building if the cracks in the walls and holes in the floorboards are anything to go from. How has this place not been shut down?

"Please write your names and sign here," she says, handing me a pen.

I write both mine and Tilly's name down before I hand her back the pen. Tilly gives me a strange look, not knowing what is going on either, but we wait as the lady speaks to someone. The door to the left is opened, and a security man comes out. The man is young, with dark hair and a serious expression, and he's dressed in a blue uniform.

"This way," he says, holding the door open for us.

I walk into the large room, which is full of windows overlooking the dead grass and dead trees. The place is dark, a few of the lights need replacing, and it looks in bad shape with bits of wallpaper falling off. The room is full of old and young people, who don't look like they notice we have walked in at all. Most of the young people I see are just staring at their hands in their laps, and one girl with black hair is rocking back and forth in her seat.

I pull Tilly closer to me with my hand, and she rests her head on my arm as neither of us know what to say about the sight we are seeing. Most are talking to themselves, some are playing cards or chess in the corners of the room, but no one is talking loud. There's no noise in the room, and that's the creepy part. I turn and watch as the security man locks the door behind us.

"Which one is Julia Smith?" I ask him, and he gives me a puzzled look. I guess it must be strange to have someone turn up for a visit and not know who they are looking for.

"You're here for Julia? The woman is a little crazy so don't get too close. She tends to flip and attack visitors, and you don't want her doing that to your pretty girlfriend," he says, and I glare at him. I don't need a warning, and if Arthur was visiting this person, I respect her for trying to attack him. "Dude . . . just a warning," he says, holding his hands up.

Tilly squeezes my hand to get my attention, and I

force myself not to hurt the innocent security guard for being an idiot.

"Just show us," I say, and he nods, moving in front of us and walking through the people in the room. I stop in my tracks when I see who he is pointing at. Sitting in a chair, looking out the window, is an older version of the woman I have seen in photos. I can't remember her as a child, but I would know my own mother anywhere. Even one who left when I was a child.

"Mother," I say tightly, and I feel Tilly squeeze my hand in comfort. My mother doesn't respond as she stares out the window in a haze. I don't see anyone other than my mother as I walk forward and sit in the seat opposite her. When she finally turns to look at me, I see her green eyes and her brown hair, which has started to go grey at the top. But it's her emotionless eyes that do me in.

"Who are you?" she asks me.

"Harley King," I say, and she holds a hand out.

"Harley . . . I'm Julia, and I like your name," she says, and I shake her hand. There wasn't an ounce of recognition from her when I said my name. My mother's name isn't Julia.

"Do you not know who I am?" I ask her, letting go of Tilly's hand and kneeling down so I'm at her level, and she smiles.

"No, but you look familiar. Like a ghost," she says, and then she laughs a little. "I like ghosts," she adds, and I look over at the guard who watches us.

"I will be right back, Julia," I tell her, and she nods, looking out the window again. I stand up and move closer to Tilly, who just watches.

"I'm going to find out what I can. Will you talk with her? See if she will tell you anything?" I whisper.

"Of course," she says, knowing the story I had been told about my mother walking out on us all when I was a child. I don't believe she did, not if she can't remember us and is in a place like this. I look back once more at my mother, seeing the dazed look she is giving the window. I wonder how many drugs she is on.

"I want to know what happened to my mother to have her end up in here. I'm her next of kin, and I thought she had just walked out on us as children. Not that she is clearly not in her right mind and in a mental hospital," I tell the security guard, whose eyes widen.

"Look, I will take you to the boss. She will be the only one who can tell you anything. I've only been working here a few months, man," the guy says, holding his hands in the air. I take a deep breath and nod at him. He opens the door for me and goes to talk to the old lady behind the desk, who picks up the phone and rings someone.

"Go and watch my mother and girlfriend. If anything happens to them while I'm here, I will personally blame you," I warn the man, who gulps and quickly goes back into the room.

I pace the entrance hall for what seems like ages, but likely isn't long, until an older woman walks down the stairs behind the desk. The woman has dark-brown hair, a serious expression, and is wearing a suit.

"I'm Mrs. Banna. You are Mr. King, I believe?" she asks me, and I nod. She hands me a folder and then gestures to the seat.

"Everything we have on Miss Julia Smith is in there, but I can run through what we know if you wish?" she asks me.

"Yes." I nod curtly.

"I had just started working here when Julia was brought in. She had been found in a hospital, with no identity and a head injury. They say she was found washed up on a beach and when she woke up with no knowledge of her name, they brought her here," she tells me. I wonder what my father did to her, to have her end up on a beach with a head injury. I doubt she did it to herself, and my father was sick enough to do it.

"Why did you keep her here? If it was only a loss of memory? She isn't crazy?" I ask her, and she shakes her head at me.

"Your mother has episodes where she attacks people randomly. She wakes up in the night screaming but can't remember what was scaring her in her dreams when she wakes up. To be honest with you, if she had a family to go home to, it could happen, but until now . . ." she says, and she doesn't need to finish the sentence. She hasn't had anyone until now.

"Arthur visits her, doesn't he?" I ask.

"Yes, there's a man who visits her. He visits a lot of the people here and is just a good man–" she says with a smile.

"He is not a good man and is likely the one who put my mother in here with help from my father," I spit out, standing up. The woman looks shocked but doesn't know what to say to me.

"I will find a better place for my mother to stay; she can't be left here. I will pay for it all to be sorted and to have her close to my home. Despite who my mother was, she is my mother and my responsibility," I say, and the woman nods her understanding. "I will also be calling my private doctor to have a look at her and see what medications she should be on. She looks out of it in there," I comment.

"She is on—"

"I don't want to know. I'm leaving," I say and go to the room, banging on the door. The security man opens it up, giving me a nervous look as I walk over to Tilly and my mother. My mother is laughing a little at whatever Tilly is saying to her.

"Lovely girl," she tells Tilly, holding her hand.

"It was lovely to meet you, Julia," Tilly says.

"Come back?" she asks, but her eyes look up at me.

"I will come back, and I have some brothers who would like to meet you, if you want?" I ask her, kneeling down to her level. When I kneel, I see the large cut that goes from her forehead and into her hairline. Her dark hair covers it further, but it looks bad, even knowing its age.

"Yes. Meet more people." She nods her head excitedly, and it makes her seem more childlike than the adult she is. I smile tightly and take Tilly's hand as I straighten up.

"Bye, Julia," Tilly says.

"Bye, Tilly," she says, and then she looks back out at the window. I turn with Tilly and walk out of the room.

"Watch my mother. It's your new job, and I will pay you a fortune to make sure she is safe until she leaves here very soon," I tell the security guard, whose eyes widen, and he quickly nods.

"I will protect her for you, Mr. King," he says.

"Good man," I reply, waiting for him to open the door. When we are both sitting back in my car, I rest my head against the steering wheel.

"Did she say anything to you?" I ask Tilly, who just silently waits for me to move. Just there supporting me, knowing I need a minute.

"Nothing much. She talked about a show on TV she liked but nothing else. She kind of acts a little like a–"

"Child." I finish her sentence, looking up as she nods.

"They gave me this. But basically it says she was found washed up on a beach, with complete memory loss and a bad head injury," I say, handing her the folder.

"Harley . . . I don't know what to say."

"How am I going to tell my brothers this? The mother they hate for walking out on them, likely didn't walk out at all. It's more likely our dad got rid of her, and then Arthur kept her here to use against us at some point," I say, leaning back in my seat.

"You tell them the truth and let them make their decisions. They are adults now, Harley," she tells me, and I know she is right, but part of me still wants to protect them from this.

"I still see them as the boys I tried to protect from my father," I tell her, and she gives me a sad smile, and then her phone starts ringing in her pocket.

"It's Devon, I'm sure it can wait . . ." she says.

"No, it's okay; answer it," I tell her, and she does.

"What?" she says, her face draining of all colour before she drops the phone out of her hand and stares at me.

"Tilly?" I ask, wondering what the hell her brother just said.

"Daniel knocked my mother out and took my baby," she says in a horrified whisper. I pick the phone up off her lap.

"Devon, it's me. Call everyone and get them to my house. We have a dead man to find," I say.

## CHAPTER 27
TILLY

"Tilly?" I hear someone saying my name, but I just keep staring at the empty baby rocker in the living room, unaware of everyone moving around, the police who just came into the room, or Izzy, who is shaking my shoulder. The word 'kidnap' just keeps repeating over and over in my mind. I never should have stayed here, I knew he would find me.

"Tilly?" Harley asks, kneeling in front of me. I try to focus on him, the stress that's all over his face, but everything feels numb. I know I'm in shock, but I can't process anything other than the fact my baby is gone, and my mother is in the hospital after being knocked out.

"The police need you to tell them everything you

can about Daniel. Okay? It will help find him and find baby–"

"Hope. Her name is Hope Elizabeth King," I tell him, and there's a silence around us as I speak the first words I've said since Devon called me.

"Tilly . . ." I hear Izzy gasp, knowing my baby's middle name is after her.

"I will find our daughter, I promise you," he tells me, and if anyone else would have said that to me, I wouldn't have believed them, but Harley is different.

"Madam?" a female police officer asks, moving to sit on the other side of me and pulling out a pad and pen. "Anything you can tell me, we can use. We have every available police officer looking for him and checking every car that leaves the village. But we need to know some things," she tells me.

"I'm going to find him. I will bring Hope back home, Tilly," Harley says, and I can't speak as I watch him walk out, with Devon and Luke at his side. Sebastian, Elliot, and everyone other than Izzy is out looking. Except for my mum who is in the hospital with my father at her side.

"We spoke to your mother, she gave us a photo of Daniel. She told me that you ran away from him because he attempted to rape you, is that right?" the police officer asks once the room is empty of everyone other than Izzy and me.

"Yes. I didn't know he knew about the baby," I say in a whisper, watching as she writes things down on a pad.

"Tilly thought she saw him a few weeks ago, didn't you?" Izzy says, and I nod. I should never have stayed here, not when my family came. I should have taken Hope and ran.

"Yes. Also, I've had someone cold call me several times a day, every day. I thought it was someone selling something with a bad connection," I tell her and then burst into tears. "I'm so stupid, and Hope is gone because of me."

"This is not your fault, Tilly," Izzy says, pulling me into a hug. I let her rub my back as I haven't been able to stop crying for a long time.

"It's been hours, he could be hours away with her by now," I say, knowing we have no idea how long my mum was out, and how long he has had Hope for.

"Harley won't give up until he finds her, none of them will. Hope is a King, and we stick together," Izzy tells me as I keep sobbing.

"If it helps, Miss, we believe he didn't leave the village. Usually, men like this are obsessed with the mother as well. He might be waiting to lure you out," the officer says gently, but I can't hear her as I stand up.

"Then we go and search the village, I can't stay here," I say, smoothing my top down and picking up a tissue off the side. I wipe my eyes as Izzy stands up.

"Miss, we recommend that you stay here in case there is any news. I have to stay with you for your own protection," she tells me.

"Then come with me, I'm not staying here. If Daniel wants me, he can find me. I don't care, but I want to find my daughter," I say, knowing that staying in this house, surrounded by her things, isn't going to help me find her. Daniel is playing a game, a game to mess with me.

"Okay," the officer says, nodding. Izzy doesn't say a word as we get into my car and drive into town.

# CHAPTER 28

HARLEY

"You sure?" I ask Tilly's oldest brother, Grayson, over the phone. I wasn't surprised he had my number, as I checked the twentieth hotel we have been in today. They hadn't seen any babies, and there has been no news from the police. The police have started going door to door in the village, but I doubt he is stupid enough to stay there.

"Look, don't ask how I found out, but he is at that hotel in Blackpool. Go and get my niece back. I'm trusting you, Harley King. With everything I know about you and your family's past, I'm trusting you," he tells me, making it clear he knows a lot about my family as well. What the hell does Grayson Fox do for a living?

"You can trust me. Call Devon, as he's with the

others, and call Tilly to let her know what's going on. I'm with Luke, my brother, and close to Blackpool," I say, knowing we have been checking all the hotels all last night and all day today. It's been over forty-eight hours since he took Hope. Thank God, we have some kind of lead. The police have been useless, and Tilly sounds more desperate every time I call her.

"I know who Luke is, and I will call the others. Bring Hope home," he says, and then the line goes dead. I pull my car out of the carpark.

"Grayson says he is certain Daniel is at an old hotel near the beach in Blackpool," I say, and Luke nods.

"Let's find him then," he says, and neither of us say anything more as I drive the ten minutes it takes to get to Blackpool. We were close. I pull up outside the little hotel that is on a range of old hotels on a tiny road. It's an excellent place to hide; I'm sure the people who run it would take cash.

"I will get Hope, and you take her to the car. Daniel is mine to deal with," I tell Luke.

"Dude, I'm not going to let you kill him. This isn't The Cage, and Arthur isn't here to hide the body. You just escaped, we all did. Let's just get Hope and leave," Luke says, pulling on my arm, but I shake him off.

"I won't kill him, but he will wish I had," I spit

out and storm off up the steps of the hotel.

The entrance hall is small, with a desk and a young woman sitting behind it. She stands up when we walk in. "How can I help you? Do you have a booking?"

"No booking, but a man is staying here with a small baby. Which room?" I ask her.

"We can't give information out about customers staying here," she says, and I reach into my pocket, pulling out my wallet. I pull out the ten fifty-pound notes in there and slap it down on the desk.

"You can tell me, and take the cash. Or I can come around there and find the information I want," I tell her, having had enough of this messing around.

"Harley, calm down," Luke says, stepping in front of me.

"The baby has been kidnapped. Surely you have watched the news? The baby called Hope King who is missing?" he asks her, and she nods, pulling out the folder. She flips it open.

"Room eight, that's on the top floor. I haven't seen the baby as I only clocked in this morning and they checked in last night. But they're the only ones staying here who asked for a travel cot," she says, and I turn away to find the stairs. The hotel has four floors, which I run up as fast as I can, and I find room eight at the top.

"We should knock; he wouldn't expect that. You don't want to scare Hope," Luke says, putting a hand on my chest and stopping me.

I nod, lifting my hand and knocking on the door three times. There's a tense silence as I hear footsteps, and then the door is opened. The man standing in front of me is Daniel. I know from the research I did on him when Tilly told me she ran away from him. He is shorter than me, with blond hair, a scar near his eyebrow, and blue eyes. That's all there is to him; he looks like a regular guy, a guy you would never expect to steal a baby.

"Daniel?" I ask him, stepping closer and lifting him off the ground by his shirt. He wrestles with me, but he isn't strong enough as I slam him into the wall. I press my face close to his.

"If I didn't have a family, girlfriend, and a baby to bring up. I would kill you for this," I tell him, and he tries to pull my hands away from his shirt as it chokes him.

"She is mine, mine. You can't take my girlfriend and my baby."

"You don't force yourself on your girlfriend. You lost her and Hope when you tried to do that," I spit out.

"She wanted it. She always did." Daniel laughs,

and I bang his head into the wall as he keeps laughing. The sick fucker.

"Harley?" Luke says. I barely hear him through the haze of wanting to kill the man in my hands. Then I hear Hope crying, and everything slows down. The sound of her crying makes me step back a little, but I keep my hands on him.

"I've got him," Luke tells me, and I drop Daniel to the floor. I know Luke will sort him.

I walk into the bedroom, seeing the empty bottles on the sides, the car seat, and Hope in the travel cot. I lift her out, holding her close to me. She instantly stops crying, like she always does. I jump when I hear a male scream and then a gunshot.

"Luke?" I cry out as I run around the bed toward the hallway where Luke is standing, holding one hand to his side, where a knife is sticking out of his stomach, while his other hand holds a gun. On the floor is Daniel, with blood pouring from his neck. Luke shot him, and he won't be surviving that.

I turn Hope's face away so she can't see as I pause, not knowing what to do.

"Did you bring a gun?" I ask Luke, who nods, resting against the door.

"POLICE!" I hear shouted up the stairs, just before three police officers run up the stairs, take in the scene, and Luke falls to the ground.

## CHAPTER 29
TILLY

"Hope is okay? You have her?" I repeat again to Harley, who just told me he has Hope in his arms right now. I hear her cry a little and sink to the floor of the lounge, holding my hand over my mouth as I hold in my own cry. I feel Izzy wrap an arm around me, but everything is blurry. My baby is safe.

"She is safe and healthy. Tilly . . . you need to come to the local hospital and bring all of my brothers, and Izzy. I will text you the postcode," he tells me.

"What? Why? What's wrong with Hope?" I ask quickly.

"Nothing, Tilly. But I need you here," he tells me, his voice cracking a little.

"On our way now," I tell him.

"I love you," Harley replies.

"I love you, too," I respond before the line cuts off.

"They found Hope?" Izzy asks me.

"Yes. They are at the hospital, and Harley wanted me to get you and all your brothers there as quick as possible," I say, and she frowns, wondering what is going on as well.

The police officer who stayed with us comes running into the room. "They have found the baby," she says, and I nod, holding up my phone and standing up.

I grab my changing bag off the side, which is packed with anything Hope will need, and throw it over my shoulder. "Harley just called. He said we need to get to the hospital, so excuse us," I comment.

"Yes. Can I take you?" she asks.

"That's a good idea; we have both been awake for a long time now, and driving wouldn't be safe. We can call around and tell everyone on the way," Izzy replies before me, and I nod. She has a point. I haven't slept since Daniel took Hope.

I pick up the pink blanket I know she loves and my phone as we follow the officer to the car. Izzy gets through to Sebastian, who is with Elliot, and I call my mum, who tells all my family. It takes twenty minutes to get to the hospital as we hit some traffic on the way. I jump out of the car when she parks and run toward the hospital, with Izzy calling me as she runs to follow me.

"Harley," I say, my words only a whisper when I see him sitting in the waiting room with Hope sleeping in his arms.

I don't see the officers in the room, or anyone really, as I run over and fall to my knees in front of him. He instantly hands me Hope, and I hold her to my chest as I feel Harley wrap his arms around me and pull me onto his lap. I silently cry as I hold her close, knowing I'm never letting her out of my sight again. I wrap the pink blanket around her, and she snuggles into it.

"Thank you. Thank you. Thank you," I mutter out in a whisper, and Harley kisses my forehead.

"We need to talk, siren," he tells me gently, and I look up at him just as Sebastian and Elliot come into the room.

Izzy is standing by the door, and I see the two police officers sitting on the other side of the room as well.

"Why are we here? Where is Luke?" Elliot asks Harley.

"Luke was stabbed by Daniel, and he shot Daniel in response," Harley says, and there's silence following his words.

"Is Luke alive?" Sebastian asks, his voice cracking.

"Yes. He is in surgery now, but the police are pressing charges against him for carrying a firearm."

"That's bullshit," Elliot spits out.

"Daniel is dead. This is serious, Elliot. I've called our lawyer, but Luke will face charges for this," Harley tells them.

I feel such a sense of relief that Daniel is dead, and some small part of me shouldn't feel that way, but I do. I look down at Hope, knowing she is better off without him in her life. He was an evil man, but I hate that Luke is going to pay the price for killing him.

"He's alive, that's all that matters," Izzy tells them all.

"Alive, but going to jail," Sebastian comments.

"There's more we need to talk about," Harley tells them and then turns to the police officers. "Can we have a moment?" he asks them.

"We cannot leave you alone until you give us a statement, Mr. King."

"I'm not giving you one until my lawyer is here, but this is personal, and none of them were there. I can't see how a moment alone with my family is going to hurt anyone. You can wait outside the room." Harley waves a hand at the door and gives them a look, which would scare anyone.

The police officers quickly nod and walk out of the room, with Elliot shutting the door behind them. I try to get off Harley's lap, but he tightens his hands on my hips, telling me all I need to know . . . that he wants me here.

"What else could you tell us?" Elliot says with a groan, sitting in one of the seats opposite him. Sebastian doesn't say a word as he sits next to Elliot and Izzy sits on his other side.

"When I finished the last fight, Arthur gave me a note. He said it was a gift for me," Harley starts off.

"What was on the note?" Izzy asks.

"An address, a time, and a date. When Hope was taken, we were at the address. I know Arthur likely helped Daniel," he tells them all and then looks up at me. "I'm so sorry."

"Don't be. This wasn't your fault. And you got her back to me, to us. Our daughter is safe," I tell him, gently kissing his cheek before looking down at Hope who sleeps quietly, completely unaware of the things going on around her. I know she will never remember being stolen, her uncle being stabbed, or her biological father dying. I hate that he died before he could be arrested, before he could pay for everything he has done. Death was an easy escape for him.

"What was at the address?" Elliot asks Harley, who only tenses a little before he replies quickly.

"Our mother."

"What?" Elliot shouts, waking Hope up. She starts grumbling a little, and I slide off Harley's lap, gently rocking her.

"She isn't well. I don't think she ever walked out on us," Harley tells them. Sebastian looks at the floor, and Elliot just shakes his head.

"You can't believe that, Harley," Elliot says.

"Tell us everything," Sebastian says, placing a hand on Elliot's shoulder.

"I'm going to find her some milk," I tell Harley, who gives me a nod. I walk out of the room and shut the door behind me, just as Allie and Emilia come running down the corridor.

"I heard something happened to Luke," Emilia says, panic all over her face.

"Is Elliot in there? I'm so happy you have Hope back," Allie says, giving me a small smile.

"Luke has been stabbed and is in surgery. I don't know anything else. Elliot, Sebastian, Izzy, and Harley are having a talk in there. I would leave them for a little bit," I respond, answering all their questions. Emilia runs around me and straight toward the reception desk.

"Do you need anything?" Allie asks me, wrapping an arm around my shoulders.

I look back at the door, giving her the only answer I can. "I want everyone to be okay."

"Me, too," Allie whispers.

# CHAPTER 30

## HARLEY

"To what do I owe the pleasure?" Arthur laughs as I walk into the office at the back of The Cage.

I slam the door shut and walk across the room. Arthur tries to pull the drawer to his desk open, to, no doubt, get a weapon out, but I get to him first. I slam my fist into his face, sending him flying from his chair, and I lean down, picking him up and slamming him onto the desk. I wrap my hands around his neck and start squeezing. He struggles against me, trying to move my hands and mouthing words I'm not listening to. I loosen my hands a little and move closer.

"You may think you're indestructible in here, but this is proof you are not. I know what you did, I know you helped that shit-head, Daniel. That my brother is in court tomorrow because of you. That my girlfriend went through hell because of you." I lean closer. "Why shouldn't I kill you? Get rid of your pathetic existence?" I say then let go, and he slides off the desk. I stand, looking down at him as he gasps for breath.

"I . . . I will leave you alone. Nothing more from me," he gasps out, and I laugh as I pull the gun out of my jacket. I unlock the safety and point the gun at his head.

"You spent years trying to make my brothers like our father and me, but you never realised that if you succeeded, it was likely I would kill you. My father tried to kill you because he was stupid, and you're lucky I'm not."

"Thank . . . y-you," he says, and I lean down, placing the gun next to his head. He goes very still.

"But, Arthur, I'm not fucking around. Now, you mess with my family once more, in any way, and I'm going to kill you." I push the gun into his head, making him lean his head to the side. "And, it won't be quick."

"I get it," he says, and I stand up.

"One more thing, I want you to leave this town. If I see you around, you're dead. That's your price for everything. I know you have other businesses," I say, and he nods, rubbing his swollen neck.

I walk out of the office, slamming the door behind me and looking down at the four, knocked-out guards outside the room. Sebastian and Elliot are leaning against the entrance to The Cage. I slide my gun back into my pocket as I step over one of the men and walk toward my brothers.

"Alive?" Elliot asks.

"Yes, but he gets it. We won't be seeing Arthur again," I tell them both.

We walk out of The Cage and get into my car before making the ten-minute trip to the nursing home I've put our mother into.

"You sure you both want to do this?" I ask them as I turn the car off.

"I am," Sebastian says, getting out of the car.

"Elliot?" I ask him as he stares at the building.

"I'm staying in the car. I just can't see her. I know what you told me. I know she didn't leave me, but I need Allie here. I just can't," he says, shaking his head. I place my hand on his shoulder.

"I get it. No matter what, she will be here for a long time, and you can meet her when you want to," I tell him.

"Go." He nods his head toward where Sebastian is waiting outside the nursing home.

The nursing home is a brick building, which only has twenty people living here and twenty-four-seven care for my mother. The outside is lined with flowers, the windows don't have horrible bars on them, and overall, it's nice.

"Elliot isn't coming in?" Sebastian asks, and I give him a nod for an answer. I don't have to say anything else, this is hard enough for all of us.

"Mr. King, she is waiting for you," Susan, a middle-aged nurse, says as she stands up from behind the counter in the entrance hall.

"Lovely to see you, Susan."

"You must be one of the other sons she tells me about; Sebastian, Elliot, or Luke?"

"Sebastian," he answers.

"What has she said?" I ask Susan.

"Well, since we have weaned her off that high amount of drugs she was on, she never stops talking. She tells me stories of you as babies, what you liked to play with."

"So she is normal?"

"Normal is a complicated word. You mother still has episodes where she gets petrified, and we have to sedate her. I hope, with time, there will be less and less," she tells Sebastian, who gives her a tight nod. We all have an idea of what happened to frighten her so much and cause these episodes. It must have been something our father did.

"How are your lovely girlfriend and baby

doing?" she asks me. We brought Hope here last week to see my mother, Tilly and I.

"What normal three-month-olds do, chew everything and never stop eating," I chuckle, loving how Hope is far more settled at home with Tilly and me.

Following the weeks after she was taken, she was not sleeping and seemed unsettled, but I think it was because Tilly was so on edge and watching her all the time. When Tilly started to relax, so did Hope.

"He means the baby, I'm sure that's not what Tilly does but who knows what goes on behind closed doors," Sebastian says, making her laugh, and I glare at him. "Lighten up, bro," he says, hitting my arm.

Susan opens a door for us. "She is in here and having a good day."

"You ready for this?" I ask Sebastian, who nods.

"I'm a King, and you taught me how to be ready for anything," he says with a smirk, walking in.

# EPILOGUE

## LUKE- 5 YEARS LATER.

I get out of my car, slamming the door shut and looking up at the house I haven't seen in five long years. Everything has changed, but the house still looks the same. The same brick walls and large windows, the same front door. I pull my suit jacket on and walk up to the door. I lift my hand, knocking on the door of my old home. I don't think I've ever knocked before.

"Luke?" Maisy asks as she opens the door, shock all over her face.

Maisy doesn't look older, she is still beautiful with long, black hair and big, blue eyes. She holds the door open as I walk in, and she stands, keeping it open and not saying a word. The last time I saw her was with all my family when I was charged and went to prison for two years. Not that I spent the whole two years there; I never did. Only, the price of being out of jail early was never seeing my family. Pretending I hated them all. Pretending for five years to be someone I'm not.

"Who is it?" I hear my sister shout just before she walks out of the living room in her wedding dress. Her long, blond hair is up in a complicated bun, and her long, white dress looks amazing on her. I've seen photos of them all over the years, but it's still strange to see her so grown up.

"Luke?" she whispers, dropping the flowers she was holding to the ground before running over to me and wrapping her arms around my neck. I let her hug me for a second before stepping away. "Where the hell have you been? It's been five years since . . ." she says, her green eyes locked onto mine.

"Izzzzzyyy!" I hear a male child's voice, and then I look up to see a small, dark-haired boy running down the stairs, with a little red haired girl next to him. They look the same age, but I don't know who he is. I recognise the five-year-old girl as Hope, but the boy isn't Jake, the only boy in the family. I've kept my eye on them all enough to know what they look like. The boy and Hope run over to Izzy, both of them dressed for the wedding.

"Luke . . . what the hell?" Harley asks, walking down the stairs and stopping on the last step as we stare at each other. Harley has cut his hair, it's shorter and stops around his ears now and shorter at the front. All the years of being married and having Hope to look after has made him look happy. I saw photos of their wedding in Spain. It was just him, Tilly, and Hope.

"I know I have a lot to explain, but I wouldn't miss my sister's wedding," I reply with a small smile.

Thank you so much for reading Fall!! A big thank you to Helayna, Mads and everyone that supported me with this book!

A special shout out the to lovely designer, Daqri, and the photographer, Sara!!

Thank you and if you have a second, a review would be amazing! They are everything to authors, even if it's just a quick "I like this book."

Thank you for your continued support! You're all amazing!

# **EXCLUSIVE EXTRA SCENE OF WHEN BLAKE PROPOSES TO IZZY...**

IZZY

I pull Blake's shirt over my head, as it's getting a little cold in here despite the fire and all of the candles. I pull my hair out through the shirt, then Blake's phone starts ringing in his jacket. I know I should answer it in case it's important, as my phone has gone flat. I pick his jacket up, feeling around, and something falls out, banging on the floor as the phone stops ringing. I put the jacket down and lean down to pick the box up, pausing when I look at the white ring box.

*It couldn't be?*

I look up as Blake opens the door and stops in his tracks when he sees me holding the box. Blake hasn't got a shirt on, just his black jeans, and he looks amazing with his messy, blond hair. I never think he looks bad, even when I'm looking after him when he is sick. Blake is too handsome, but I love him. I love him so much.

"This isn't what I planned, but I've given up on planning anything now," Blake says when he walks through the door and puts the candles down on the sofa. Blake walks straight over to me, gently taking the box from me and kneeling down on one leg.

"I think the best way is to start off by being honest. I've been planning this for months, and every big date I've taken you on, I intended to propose. I wanted to propose at the beach, on the boat, at the picnic, and I could just go on and on." He chuckles.

"Oh my god, they all went so wrong." I gasp, and he laughs.

"Yes, but it's not going to stop me from asking you to marry me, Izzy. When I met you, your big, green eyes, soft, blond hair, and feisty attitude drew me in. I knew straight away that I'd be the luckiest man if you gave me a chance to be with you. We went through so much, and it was never easy to be together, but we didn't give up. I couldn't have given up on you if I tried, Izzy. I love you, more than I ever thought it was possible to love someone." He pauses as I wipe my eyes, and he opens the box. I look down at the large diamond in the middle, and the sapphires on the other side.

"Sapphires, like my necklace," I comment, not believing that he did that for me.

"Yes. I know you miss your mother, and I couldn't think of a more perfect way to have her remembered."

"Blake," I whisper.

"Elizabeth King, will you marry me?" he asks, and I pick the ring up out of the box, sliding it onto my finger and meeting his blue eyes.

"Yes."

## LEAVING THE PAST BEHIND.

### ANASTASIA

I stand still on the side of the train tracks, letting the cold wind blow my blonde and purple dip-dyed hair across my face. I squeeze the handle of my suitcase tighter, hoping that the train will come soon. *It's freezing today, and my coat is packed away in the suitcase, dammit.* I feel like I've waited for this day for years, the day I get to leave my foster home and join my sister at college. I look behind me into the parking lot, seeing my younger sister stood watching me go, my foster grandmother holding her hand.

Phoebe is only eleven years old, but she is acting strong today, no matter how much she wants me to stay. I smile at her, trying to ignore how difficult it feels to leave her here, but I know she couldn't be in a better home. I can get through college with our older sister and then get a job in the city, while living all together. *That's the plan anyway.*

We lost our mum and dad in a car accident ten years ago, and we were more than lucky to find a foster parent that would take all three of us in. Grandma Pops is a special kind of lady. She is kind and loves to cook, and the money she gets from fostering pays for her house. She lost her two children in a fire years ago, and she tells us regularly that we keep her happy and alive. Even if we do eat a lot for three kids. Luckily, she likes to look after us as I burn everything I attempt to cook. And I don't even want to remember the time I tried to wash my clothes, which ended in disaster.

"Train four-one-nine to Liverpool is calling at the station in one minute," the man announces over the loudspeaker, just before I hear the sound of the train coming in from a distance. I turn back to see the grey train speeding towards us, only slowing down when it gets close, but I still have to walk to get to the end carriage. I wait for the two men in front of me to get on before I step onto the carriage, turning to pull my suitcase on. I search through the full seats until I find an empty one near the back, next to a window. I have to make sure it's facing the way the train is going as it freaks me out to sit the other way. I slide my suitcase under the seat before sitting down, leaving my handbag on the small table in front of me.

I wave goodbye to my sister, who waves back, her head hidden on grandma's shoulder as she cries. I can only see her waist length, wavy blonde hair before the train pulls away. I'm going to miss her. *Urgh, it's not like we don't have phones and FaceTime!* I'm being silly. I pull my phone out of my bag and quickly send a message to my older sis, letting her know I am on the train. I also send a message to Phoebe, telling her how much I love and miss her already.

"Ticket?" the train employee guy asks, making me jump out of my skin, and my phone falls on the floor.

"Sorry! I'm always dropping stuff," I say, and the man just stares at me with a serious expression, still holding his hand out. His uniform is crisply ironed, and his hair is combed to the left without a single hair out of place. I roll my eyes and pull my bag open, pulling out my ticket and handing it to him. After he checks it for about a minute, he scribbles on it before handing it back to me. I've never understood why they bother drawing on the tickets when the machines check the tickets at the other end anyway. I put my ticket back into my bag before sliding it under the seat just as the train moves, jolting me a little.

I reach for my phone, which is stuck to some paper underneath it. I've always been taught to pick up rubbish, so I grab the paper as well as my phone before slipping out from under the table and back to my seat. I put my phone back into my handbag before looking at the leaflet I've picked up. It's one of those warning leaflets about familiars and how it is illegal to hide one. The leaflet has a giant lion symbol at the top and warning signs around the edges. It explains that you have to call the police and report them if you find one.

Familiars account for 0.003 percent of the human race, though many say they are nothing like humans and don't like to count them as such. Familiars randomly started appearing about fifty years ago, or at least publicly they did. A lot of people believe they just kept themselves hidden before that. The Familiar Empire was soon set up, and it is the only place safe for familiars to live in peace. They have their own laws, an alliance with humans, and their own land in Scotland, Spain and North America.

Unfortunately, anyone could suddenly become a

familiar, and you wouldn't know until one random day. It can be anything from a car crash to simply waking up that sets off the gene, but once a familiar, always a familiar. They have the mark on their hand, a glowing tattoo of whatever animal is bonded to them. The animals are the main reason familiars are so dangerous. They have a bond with one animal who would do anything for them. Even kill. And I heard once that some kid's animal was a lion as big as an elephant. But those are just the things we know publicly, who knows what is hidden behind the giant walls of the Familiar Empire?

"My uncle is one, you know?" a girl says, and I look up to see a young girl about ten years old hanging over her seat, her head tilted to the side as she stares at the leaflet in my hand. "He has a big rabbit for a familiar."

"That's awesome..." I say, smiling as I put the leaflet down. I bet picking up giant rabbit poo isn't that awesome, but I don't tell her that.

"I want to be a familiar when I grow up," she excitedly says. "They have cool powers and pets! Mum won't even let me get a dog!"

"Sit down, Clara! Stop talking to strangers!" her mum says, tugging the girl's arm, and she sits down after flashing me a cheeky grin.

I fold the leaflet and slide it into my bag before

resting back in the seat, watching the city flash by from the window. I couldn't think of anything worse than being a familiar. You have to leave your family, your whole life, and live in the woods. *Being a familiar seems like nothing but a curse.*

## WHO WEARS A CLOAK THESE DAYS?

"Ana!!" my sister practically screeches as I step off the train, and then throws herself at me before I get a second to really look at her. Even though my sister is only a few inches taller than my five-foot-four self, she nearly knocks me over. I pull her blonde hair away from my face as it tries to suffocate me before she thankfully pulls away. I'm not a hugger, but Bethany always ignores that little fact.

"I missed you too, Bethany," I mutter, and she grins at me. Bethany was always the beautiful sister, and as we got older, she just got prettier. Seems the year at college has only added to that. Her blonde hair is almost white, falling in perfect waves down her back. Mine is the same, but I dyed the ends a deep purple. Another one of my attempts at sticking out in a crowd when I usually become invisible next to my gorgeous sister. Phoebe is the image of Bethany, and both of them look like photos of our mother. Whereas I look like my dad mostly, I still have the blonde hair. Bethany grins at me, then slowly runs her eyes over my outfit before letting out a long sigh.

"You look so pretty, sis," she says, and I roll my eyes. Bethany hates jeans and long-sleeved tops, which I happen to be wearing both. I didn't even look at what I threw on this morning. I shiver as the cold wind blows around me, reminding me that I should have gotten my coat out my suitcase on the train trip. It is autumn.

"You're such a bad liar," I reply, arching an eyebrow at her, and she laughs.

"Well, you are eighteen now, and I've never seen you in a dress. College is going to change all that." She waves a hand like she has sorted all the problems out.

"How so? I'm not wearing a dress to classes," I say, frowning at her. "Leggings are much easier to run around in, I think."

"Parties, of course," she tuts, laughing like it should be obvious. Bethany grabs hold of my suitcase before walking down the now empty sidewalk to the parking lot at the end.

"I need to study. There is no way I'm going to ace my nursing classes without a lot of studying," I tell her. Bethany took drama, and I wasn't the least bit surprised when she was offered a job at the end of her course, depending on her grades. Though she was an A-star student throughout high school, so there is no way she could fail.

"I love that you will have the same job mum did," she eventually tells me, and I glance over at her as she smiles sadly at me before focusing back on where she is walking. I remember my mum and dad, whereas Bethany is just over one year older than me and remembers a lot more. Phoebe doesn't remember them at all; she only has our photos and the things we can tell her. It was difficult for Bethany to leave us both to come to college, but grandma and I told her she had to find a future.

"I doubt I will do it as well as her...but I like to help people. I know this is the right thing for me to do," I reply, and I see her nod in the corner of my eye. I quickly walk forward and hold the metal gate to the car park open for Bethany to walk through before catching up with her as we walk past cars.

"You've always been the nice one. I remember when you were twelve, and the boy down the road broke up with you because some other girl asked him out. The next day, that boy fell off his bike, cutting all his leg just outside our home. You helped him into the house, put plasters on his leg, and then walked his bike back to his house for him," she remarks. "Most people wouldn't have done that. I would have just laughed at him before leaving him on the sidewalk."

"I also called him a dumbass," I say, laughing at the memory of his shocked face. "So I wasn't all that nice."

"That's why you are so amazing, sis," she laughs, and I chuckle as we get to Bethany's car. It's a run down, black Ford Fiesta, but I know Bethany adores the old thing. Even if there are scratches and bumps all over the poor car from Bethany's terrible driving.

"Get in, I can put the suitcase in the boot," she says, and I pull the passenger door open before sliding inside. I do my seatbelt up before resting back, watching out of the passenger window at the train pulling out of the station. There is a man in a black cloak stood still in the middle of the path, the wind pushing his cloak around his legs, but his hood is up, covering his face. I just stare, feeling stranger and more freaked out by the second as the man lifts his head. I see a flash of yellow under his hood for a brief moment, and I sit forward, trying to see more of the strange man I can't pull my eyes from. I almost jump out of my skin when Bethany gets in the car, slamming her door shut behind her, and I look over at her.

"Are you okay? You look pale," she asks, reaching over to put her hand on my head to check my temperature before pulling it away. I look back towards the man, seeing that he and the train are gone. Everything is quiet, still and creepy. *Time to go.*

"Yeah, everything is fine. I'm just nervous about my first day," I tell her, which is sort of honest, but I'm missing the little fact about the weird hooded man. *I mean, who walks around in cloaks like friggin' Darth Vader?* She frowns at me, seeing through my lies easily, but after I don't say a word for a while, she drops it.

"It will be fine. Don't worry!" she says, reaching over to squeeze my hand before starting the car. I keep my eyes on the spot the man was in until I can't see it anymore. I close my eyes and shake my head, knowing it was just a creepy guy, and I need to forget it. This is my first day of my new life, and nothing is going to ruin that.

## ONE MOMENT CAN CHANGE EVERYTHING.

"Anastasia Noble?" I hear someone shout out as I wait in the middle of the crowd of new students. Bethany left me here about half an hour ago, and she is going to find me later once I have my room sorted. First, I have to get through a tour of the university, even though I had a tour here when I visited two months ago. I also spent days studying the map they gave me, so I know where I am going. Putting my hand in the air, I move through the crowd, pulling my suitcase behind me with my arm starting to ache from lugging the giant purple suitcase everywhere.

I get to the front of the crowd, where an older man waves me over. I quickly make my way to him and the three other students waiting at his side. Two of them are girls, both blonde and whispering between themselves with their pink suitcases. The other is a guy who is too interested in ogling the blondes to notice me coming over. Story of my life right there. I stop right in front of the older man who stinks of too much cologne, and I shake his slightly sweaty hand before stepping back.

"Welcome to Liverpool University. We are the smallest, but fiercest, university in northern England. Now, I am going to show you around the basic area before taking you to your rooms. You all will share a corridor and living area, so look around at your new friends and maybe say hello!" the man says, clapping his hands together before quickly turning to walk away. We all jog to catch up with him as he walks us across the grass towards one of the buildings on either side of the clearing.

There is a little river in the middle with planted flowers and trees all surrounding it. It's peaceful, exactly why my sister chose this university, I suspect. She always likes seeing the beauty in life, where I am always looking for a way to fix the world instead. I wish we had other family around that could tell us about what our parents were like, who each of us follow, or if we are just random in the family line of personalities. We don't even know if our parents had any close friends. There is nothing much in our foster pack given to grandma from social services. Bethany and I talked about going to the village we lived in to ask around, but neither of us ever found the time.

"Anastasia, right?" a guy asks, slowing down to walk at my side. He has messy brown hair, blue eyes, and a big rucksack on his back.

"Yep, who are you?" I ask.

"Don. Nice to meet you," he replies, offering me a hand to shake with a big grin. I shake his hand before looking up at the massive archway we are walking through to get inside of the building. It is two smooth pillars meeting together in the middle. There are old gargoyle statues lining the archway, their creepy eyes staring down at me. Those statues always creep me out. Bethany thinks it's funny, so last Christmas, she got me gargoyle romance books as a joke. Jokes on her though; some of those books were damn good. I quickly look away, back to where we are walking, as Don starts talking again.

"I've heard there is a party tonight to welcome freshers. Are you going?" he asks me, his arm annoyingly brushing against mine with how closely he has decided to walk. I glance up at him to see his gaze is firmly focused on my breasts rather than my face.

"No. I need to unpack," I curtly reply.

"Can't it wait one night?" he asks, and I look over at him once again. He is gorgeous, but the whiney attitude about a party is a big turn off. "I will make sure you have fun."

"No. It can't wait, and I doubt anything you could do would make the party fun for me," I say honestly, and not shockingly, he nods before catching up with the two blonde girls in the group, trying his pickup techniques on them. *Men*.

Bethany says I'm picky, but actually, it's just because the general male population at my age are idiots and act like kids most of the time too. I don't see how anyone could want to date them, though Bethany is on her twelfth boyfriend since she came to college, so I know she doesn't share my opinion. She swears she will know when the right guy comes along, and it will be the same for me. I doubt it. Anyway, finding the "right" guy is not the most important thing at the moment; passing college and getting my nursing degree is.

"This is the oldest part of the university and where most the lessons are. In the welcome packs sent to your old homes were the links to an app which is a map. It will help you find your lessons," the tour guide explains before opening a door out of the old corridor and into another one which is more modern. There are white-tiled floors, lockers lining the walls, and spotlights in the ceiling that shine so brightly everything gleams. "Every student gets a locker here, which is perfect for storing books and anything you don't need for every class. Trust me, you will get a lot of books, so the lockers are a godsend."

We walk down the corridor, listening to the guide explain the history of the university when suddenly there is a burning feeling in my hand that comes out of nowhere. I scream, dropping to my knees as I grab my hand, trying to stop the incredible pain. I rub at my pale skin as it burns hot, yet there is nothing there to see. The pain gets worse until I can't see or hear anything for a moment, and I fall back. When I blink my eyes open, I'm lying on the cold floor, hearing the chatter of students near me. No one is helping me, oddly enough, and they sound like they are far away. Every part of my body hurts, aches like I've been running a marathon.

"She's a familiar. Has anyone called the police?" one person asks as I stare up at the flickering spotlight right above me.

"We should leave; she could hurt us. Who knows where her creature is!" another man harshly whispers. I lift my hand above my face almost in slow motion. My eyes widen in pure shock at the huge, glowing, purple wolf tattoo covering the back of my hand where it burned. It stops at my wrist, the wolf's fur extending halfway up my fingers and thumb. The eyes of the wolf tattoo glow the brightest as I realise what this means.

"I'm a familiar."

## TIME TO RUN BEFORE IT IS TOO LATE.

As soon as I've said it out loud, it feels like I can't breathe as I sit up and look around at the people staring at me. The group I was with are huddled by the lockers a good distance away from me now, and I turn to see more people have shown up, a few of them on their phones. All of them are scared, worried what I will do as they keep their eyes on me. They are going to call the police and have me taken away because of this. *I have to get to Bethany first.* I have to at least say goodbye to her before they come for me and take me some place where I may never see her again.

I quickly scramble to my feet and run down the corridor, passing everyone who shouts for me to stop, until I get to the door at the end. I push it open, running through the arch and into the empty clearing. Stopping by the river, I look up and quickly try to remember how to get to the dorms. Shit, I don't even know what room she is in. I pull my handbag off my shoulder to get my phone out just as I hear a low growl from right behind me.

I slowly drop my bag onto the floor and turn around, seeing a giant wolf inches away from my face. The wolf is taller than I am; its head is leant down so I can see into its stunning blue eyes. They remind me of my own eyes, to be honest, with little swirls of black, light and dark blues, all mixed together. My body and mind seem to relax as I stare at the creature, one which I should be terrified of… but I am not. I feel myself moving my hand up, and then the wolf growls a little, shaking me out of that thought.

I step back, which only seems to piss her or him off more. Some deep part of me knows I have to touch the wolf now, or I will always regret it. I take a deep breath before stepping closer and quickly placing my hand on the middle of the wolf's forehead. I didn't notice it was my hand with the familiar mark on it until this point, until it glows so brightly purple that I have to turn my head away. When the light dims, I look back to see the black wolf staring at me as I lower my hand.

"Your name is Shadow," I say out loud, though I don't have a clue how I know that, but I know it is true. Shadow bows his head before lying on the ground in front of me. He is my familiar. *That's how I know.* That's why I am not scared of the enormous wolf like I should be. I have a gigantic wolf for my familiar. *Holy crap.* It takes me a few seconds to pull my gaze from Shadow and remember what I was going to do. Find my sister, that's what.

"We need to find my sister…can you help me? Like smell her, maybe? She smells like me," I ask Shadow and then realise I have no clue if he can understand me. Shadow looks up, tilting his head to the side before stretching out, knocking his head into my stomach. I step back, sighing. "Never mind."

Shadow growls at me, and I give him a questioning look. What is up with the growling? I thought familiar animals were meant to be familiars' best friends or something. I really get the feeling Shadow isn't all that impressed with me. He shakes his giant head before walking around me and slowly running off in the direction of the other building.

"Wait up!" I have to run fast to catch up with him as he gets to the front of the university, people moving fast out of his way and some even screaming. I don't even blame them. A giant black wolf running towards you is not something you see every day. I run faster, getting to Shadow's side as we round a corner, and I hear Bethany's laugh just before I see her sat on a bench with a guy. They both turn with wide, scared eyes to us, and the guy falls back off the bench before running away.

The sounds of people's screaming, shouting and general fear drift into nothing but silence as I meet my sister's eyes as she stands up. A tear streams down her cheek, saying everything neither one of us can speak. I will be made to leave her, and I have no idea when—if ever—I will get to see her again. Bethany is the first to move, running to me and wrapping her arms around my shoulders. She doesn't even look at Shadow; she doesn't fear me either, which is a huge relief. I hug her back, trying to commit every part of her to my memory as I try not to cry. *I have to be strong.* If I break down now, Bethany will never be able to cope. I pull back as I hear sirens in the background and know my time here is coming to an end.

"I will find a way back to you. I will never stop until I do. Just look after yourself and Phoebe. Promise me?" I ask Bethany, holding my hands on her shoulders as she sobs.

"I promise. If anyone can work out a way around the rules, it's you. I love you, sis," she says, crying her eyes out between each word. I hug her once more before stepping back to Shadow's side, away from my sister and my old life. "Be safe."

"Go. Just go, I don't want you to see me arrested or how nasty the police are to familiars. The YouTube videos are enough," I say, but Bethany shakes her head, wiping her cheeks and crossing her arms. I've accidently seen enough videos online to know that the police, the government and the general population are not nice to new familiars. That's why they are taken straight away. I'm not going to fight or try to run like some familiars do. I doubt I would get far with Shadow at my side.

"I am staying until they take you. You will not be alone," she says as I hear shouting and the sounds of dozens of feet running towards us. I gasp as I feel a sharp prick in the side of my neck, and Bethany screams. Shadow growls, which turns into a howl as I try to reach for him as he falls to the ground at my side. The world turns to blackness, and the last thing I hear is Bethany's pleas for someone to leave me alone.